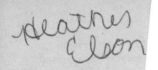

WRONG KIND OF GIRL

"You'd better keep an eye on your brother, Helen," Jessica hissed.

"What?" Helen said, looking toward the stands. Tim and Annie were standing close together.

"Do you see who he's with?"

"Annie Whitman?"

"Don't you care if your brother runs around with the school tramp?" Jessica snapped.

Helen Bradley frowned unhappily as she watched Tim and Annie leaving the gym together. "I have heard the rumors," she said.

"They aren't rumors," Jessica said, and to herself she made a vow: *Easy Annie will never be on the cheerleading squad, and that's final!*

Bantam Books in the Sweet Valley High Series
Ask your bookseller for the books you have missed

SWEET VALLEY HIGH

WRONG KIND OF GIRL

Written by
Kate William

Created by
FRANCINE PASCAL

BANTAM BOOKS
TORONTO · NEW YORK · LONDON · SYDNEY · AUCKLAND

RL 5, IL age 12 and up

WRONG KIND OF GIRL
A Bantam Book / July 1984

Sweet Valley High is a trademark of Francine Pascal

Conceived by Francine Pascal

Produced by Cloverdale Press Inc.,
133 Fifth Avenue, New York, N.Y. 10003

Cover art by James Mathewuse

ISBN 0-553-24182-6

Published simultaneously in the United States and Canada

PRINTED IN THE UNITED STATES OF AMERICA

O   0 9 8 7 6 5 4 3 2

To Don and Char Flynn

One

As she looked over the list of girls who had signed up to try out for the cheerleading squad, Jessica Wakefield purred like a satisfied cat. As co-captain of the squad, Jessica felt she was where she belonged—in charge of everything. Strictly speaking, Robin Wilson was also a co-captain, but Jessica had been heading the squad longer, and Robin pretty much let Jessica run things as she wished.

"Look at all these names!" Jessica told her twin sister Elizabeth. "Everybody wants to be a cheerleader."

It seemed perfectly logical to Jessica, of course. The cheerleaders at Sweet Valley High were the cream of the crop—the prettiest, most sought-after girls not only in the school but in the entire town of Sweet Valley, California. They included Robin Wilson, the current Miss Sweet Valley High; Helen Bradley, a stunning redhead; Jean West, a pixie brunette; and Maria Santelli, who could do back flips that took everyone's breath away. Finally, there was Jessica, who at five feet six, with a crown of glorious, sun-streaked blond hair, and those sparkling blue-green eyes, was the envy of most of the girls of Sweet Valley High.

Of course, looks were only part of it. It took more than that to make the Sweet Valley High cheering squad. You had to keep your grades up—although Jessica was the first to admit that studying wasn't her idea of world-class fun. And it didn't stop there. The cheerleaders had some indefinable style, at least the cheerleaders who could make Jessica's squad. A Sweet Valley cheerleader had to set an example for those around her. Above all, she had to have talent. Every girl on the squad was exceptional, and Jessica meant to keep it that way.

Jessica surveyed the list and waited for Elizabeth to realize the importance of the situation. Though the sisters looked exactly alike, even down to the tiny dimple in the same spot on their left cheeks, their interests were worlds apart. Jessica had tried over and over again to interest Elizabeth in the cheerleading squad. "The two of us together would be sensational!" she'd told Elizabeth at least a hundred and thirty-seven times.

But no. Where Jessica was the performer, Elizabeth was the writer. Everyone at Sweet Valley looked forward to reading Elizabeth's "Eyes and Ears" column in the school paper for the latest gossip. Her column was witty and funny and always on the mark. But never cruel. That's how Elizabeth was. And though Jessica might not always admit as much, she thought it was terrific to have a star columnist in the family.

But right then Jessica studied her sister with growing impatience. Sprawled across Elizabeth's bed, she gave a loud sigh. Her own bed and bedroom appeared as if they had been devastated by an earthquake. One of these days, Jessica was going to straighten things up. But for the moment she was too busy, and Elizabeth's bed was handy.

"Liz, how am I ever going to pick two girls out of seventy-five? Liz? *Elizabeth Wakefield!*"

Elizabeth calmly continued to brush her hair. "You called, Jess?"

"Really, Liz," Jessica wailed, "haven't you even the tiniest bit of school spirit?"

"Jess, you just broke my eardrum with your Kansas cyclone imitation, but I'm afraid I didn't get any details. What school spirit? What are you talking about?"

"The cheerleader selection, of course! Why do *I* always have to do everything myself?"

"Why? Because if anyone tried to do it, you'd be after her with a flame thrower."

"I *happen* to be co-captain. It's my responsibility."

"Yes, but there's no need to go overboard. There are five cheerleaders, and they all have a vote. You don't have to choose all by yourself."

Jessica frowned and made a face. "There's such a thing as tradition, you know. The co-

3

captain has to help the others decide. They look up to me; I can't let them down. They'll all want to know who *I* think should be picked. And look at this," she screeched, flapping the paper again. "Seventy-five girls, three tryout sessions, and only two places to fill."

"Two?" Elizabeth echoed, giving Jessica a questioning look.

"Well, yes. We have five on the team now, and there are two vacancies."

"Jessica," said Elizabeth, "didn't you promise one of those spots to Cara Walker?"

Jessica shifted uncomfortably. "Cara is a perfect choice."

"Yes, and your very best friend."

"That's beside the point. She was a terrific cheerleader before, and she's going to be terrific again. If only she and Lila hadn't gone and pulled that dumb stunt . . ."

Cara and beautiful, wealthy Lila Fowler had once been on the cheering squad but were thrown off during a big game against Palisades High. They'd sabotaged the Palisades' cheering display by turning on the school sprinkler system in the middle of their performance. The two girls were finally off probation, and eligible for the squad once more, though Lila swore she would never crawl back to the team after being humiliated by the school officials. Cara, on the other hand, couldn't wait to get back into her uniform, and all the glory that went with it, despite having to face tryouts all over again. Jessica thought Cara was sure to get on the squad again. The competition might be good, but Cara was pretty and graceful. And she already knew the ropes, which was just one more thing in her favor.

"Anyway," Jessica continued, "Cara's got all the talent a cheerleader needs."

"Especially since she's your best friend."

Jessica sat up and glared at her twin. "What are you suggesting, Liz?"

"I'm suggesting that you've made up your mind about one girl already. So you only have to choose one more."

"Cara hasn't been selected yet," Jessica said defensively. "She has to try out like anybody else."

"Oh," said Elizabeth. "Well, then, you *do* have a stupendous job. Selecting two girls. Hmmm! Now, let's see. If Cara doesn't make it—"

"But Cara *will* make it," Jessica interrupted. "I know it."

"Then you only have one to pick."

Jessica sighed and fell back on the bed. "You just don't understand." She held the sheet of paper up again and went over the list of names.

"Sandra Bacon—she's good."

Suddenly Jessica squealed and flopped over onto her stomach. "What's *this*?"

"What?" Elizabeth asked.

"I *don't* believe it!"

"What?"

"The nerve! The absolute, colossal nerve! Do you know who's put her name in?"

5

"Must be frightful," said Elizabeth.

"Annie Whitman!"

"You knew she was going to try out. She told you so."

Jessica stared at the tryout list, her eyes burning into the offending name on the paper. "How do you like that? I never thought she'd *really* be brazen enough to do it."

Elizabeth slumped back in her chair and shook her head. Her sister could be so dramatic. Jessica knew perfectly well that Annie Whitman wanted to be a cheerleader. She was always at practices, watching the Sweet Valley cheerleaders do their routines. She'd told Jessica and Elizabeth endless times that she couldn't wait to try out. And now Jessica was acting as though a house had fallen on her.

"Jess, you know I helped Annie with her math so she could get her grades up and get off probation. I told you the reason she did it was to try out for the cheerleading squad."

"I hope you didn't encourage her," Jessica said coldly.

"Encourage her? Listen, the Los Angeles Rams' defensive line couldn't hold her back."

"I don't want anybody like that on my squad," Jessica said severely.

"Like what?"

"You know what they call her. Easy Annie! She's been with every guy at school."

Elizabeth, like everyone else at Sweet Valley High, had heard the rumors about Annie. It was a sad situation. Annie was one of the most beautiful girls in town, but she had a very bad reputation. She seemed to fall deeply in love with one guy after another, but each deep love never lasted more than a night or two.

"It's probably just a lot of talk. You know how guys like to brag," Elizabeth said.

"Oh, Liz, why do you always believe the best about everybody?"

"Look, I tutored her," Elizabeth said. "I happen to know her a little. And I know she's trying to change. She worked very hard to get her grades up."

"That's just too bad."

"Jessica, I hope you're at least going to give her a chance."

"She can try out. Anybody can try out."

Elizabeth examined her sister's set mouth and fixed stare. She might as well be talking to one of the stone faces on Mount Rushmore. Still, it was worth one more try.

"Jess, it may be that Annie needs this more than just about any other girl at Sweet Valley High. It could be a turning point for her. I really want you to give her a fair chance."

Well, that was certainly fine talk! Jessica thought angrily. She was on her feet in a flash, marching around. She never told Elizabeth what to write about in *The Oracle*. Well, hardly ever.

"*I'm* the captain of the cheerleaders, Liz! Not you. I'm not going to have our whole squad . . . *tainted* by Easy Annie."

"Doesn't it even matter that she's trying to

7

change? And for heaven's sake, Jessica, how bad can a fifteen-year-old sophomore girl be?"

"When are you going to stop being so goody-goody, Liz, and accept the fact that she's just plain bad?"

"How can you be so sure, Jess?"

Suddenly Jessica smiled triumphantly, and folded her arms. Elizabeth knew then and there that she'd been lured into one of her sister's ambushes.

"Because, Liz, dear, I happen to know that your little pet Annie was up to her old tricks just last night."

Elizabeth experienced a sinking sensation in her stomach. When Jessica came on like that, it meant she had the goods.

"What happened?"

"You remember that wonderful Rick Andover? The wild maniac who kidnapped us and almost got us arrested and killed at Kelly's bar? Guess who was running around with him last night?"

"How do you know?"

"I know because our very own telephone gossip, Caroline Pearce, saw them zipping past the Dairi Burger yesterday."

"For once you're wrong, Jessica," Elizabeth said firmly. "I happen to know that Annie had a very important math test this morning, and she was home studying for it."

"Studying? In Rick Andover's hot rod?"

"Caroline Pearce was mistaken."

"We'll see about that!" Jessica said, arching her eyebrows.

Later that morning, on the way to school, Elizabeth hoped against hope that Caroline Pearce had been wrong. She had to be! Annie knew that if she failed many more tests she'd be back on probation. And that would stop her from trying out for the cheerleading squad. For once in her life, sharp-eyed, evil-minded Caroline Pearce had to be wrong.

But all that day the rumor went through the corridors of the school. Elizabeth heard it again in the cafeteria at lunch.

"Easy Annie did it again."

"What happened?"

"She was out with that bum Rick Andover."

"No!"

"Yes. Everybody says she'll take just about anyone. I guess this proves it."

Despite the whispers, Elizabeth withheld judgment. That afternoon she wrote an article on the cheerleader tryouts for *The Oracle*, carefully typing out all seventy-five names.

"Competition for the cheerleader tryouts is the greatest in the school's history," she wrote. "Good luck, everybody."

Elizabeth had left the *Oracle* office and was heading out through the front door, between the massive stone columns that adorned the building, when she spotted Annie Whitman.

She almost turned away to avoid the other girl, but something wouldn't let her. Elizabeth had to know.

"Annie," she called out. "Wait up."

Annie looked back, saw Elizabeth, and quickened her step as if to hurry away. She looked down at her shoes, and suddenly tears welled up in her eyes and rolled down her cheeks. When Elizabeth caught up with her, Annie could barely speak.

"What's the matter?" Elizabeth said softly. "Are you all right?"

Annie shook her head sorrowfully. "No, Liz, I'm not all right at all."

"What happened?"

"Who does Ms. Taylor think she is, anyway?" Annie cried.

"Your math teacher?"

"Really, Liz, it was supposed to be a little quiz, but it was more like a final."

Annie plopped down on the lawn under a huge tree, and her face looked like a dam about to burst.

"How did you do?" Elizabeth asked cautiously.

Annie let out an exasperated breath and looked away. "Rotten, of course."

"*How* rotten?"

"Oh, I think I got the first part right. Where it says write your name. After that—zilch."

Elizabeth shook her head helplessly. "You knew the test was coming."

"But I didn't realize she was going to cover everything!"

Did you study for it? Elizabeth wanted to ask but didn't.

Annie was playing with her shoelaces, untying and tying them over and over. Her hands trembled, and her eyes were red. She looked like someone who desperately needed a friend.

"I thought I knew it. I really did," she said. "I should have stayed home last night and reviewed it, I guess."

Given the opening, Elizabeth couldn't resist dashing through it. "You mean you didn't study last night?"

Annie tossed her lovely head and made a face. "I did, for a while. But I don't like to hang around the house. Anyway, Rick Andover came by and showed me his latest car. It's really neat, Liz."

Elizabeth looked at Annie. So, it was true after all. She *had* been out with Rick.

"It's a souped-up 1955 Chevy," Annie went on. "He calls it his Campbell's Special." She laughed. But as she glanced at Elizabeth, the laugh died and she fell silent.

"Don't look at me that way," Annie said.

"I'm not."

"You are!"

"Annie, I thought staying off probation was important to you."

"Oh, it is, Liz! It's just about the most important thing in my life. Because I just *have* to make the cheerleading squad, or I'll *die*. But—"

"But what?" asked Elizabeth.

"Oh, I don't know. Sometimes I think it's not even worth trying, Liz. Sometimes I feel so worthless."

"What?" Elizabeth said, truly surprised. "You?

Why, Annie, you're just about the most beautiful girl in Sweet Valley High."

A becoming blush rose in Annie Whitman's cheeks. "I am not, Liz. Oh, sometimes I think I'm sort of OK-looking, but—"

"OK-looking? Why, every boy in school is crazy about you." *Oh, no, why did I blurt that out?* Elizabeth thought miserably. But Annie didn't seem to mind. In fact, she perked up and smiled again.

"Yeah, boys like me." She giggled. "I like them, too. But I don't know," she mused. "Maybe it's because girls sometimes seem jealous of me. They're not as friendly.

"But anyway, Liz, what am I going to do about that yucky math stuff?" The gloom returned to her pretty face. "If I don't pass, I'll be back on probation, and if you're on probation, you can't go out for the cheerleader squad. Liz, the first round of tryouts is in two weeks!"

"Don't worry," Elizabeth tried to console her. "You'll make it."

Unless my darling sister has something to say about it, she added grimly to herself.

Two

Elizabeth had mixed feelings as she walked into the lobby of the apartment building where Annie and her mother lived. She had not been able to resist Annie's plea for help the day before.

Fortunately she *had* been able to get out of the house after dinner without telling Jessica where she was going. If her sister discovered she was tutoring Annie again, Elizabeth knew she would be furious. *Why am I saying "if"?* she asked herself. Jessica was sure to find out, and she'd consider it a major act of treason.

For the millionth time in her sixteen years, Elizabeth wondered how identical twins could be so different. "But I *am* doing the right thing," she said under her breath as she went up in the elevator to the fourth floor. Annie opened the door before Elizabeth even had time to ring the bell.

"Hi, Liz. Come on in! I was at the front window watching for you. You don't know how

13

much this means to me," she said breathlessly, ushering Elizabeth into the living room.

"Take it easy, Annie," Elizabeth said, laughing. "I'm only helping you with math, not saving your life."

"It's the same thing, Liz. With tryouts coming up so soon, it's absolutely the same thing."

Elizabeth wasn't surprised by the look of intensity on Annie's face, but it did make her uncomfortable. Wanting something so badly was bound to cause problems, especially with Jessica Wakefield as an opponent.

"This is a nice apartment, Annie," Elizabeth said, looking around the living room. It was small but attractive, and the furniture was ultramodern. She had never been to Annie's home before; Annie had preferred to stay after school and have Elizabeth help her.

"It's OK, I guess," Annie said, "if you like small apartments with too many people around."

"I thought it was just you and your mother."

"And Johnny makes three," Annie said bitterly.

Elizabeth stared at her blankly. Annie had a brother?

"Johnny is my mother's *very special friend*. He lives here, too. We're just one big happy family."

Elizabeth wished they had stuck to the subject of math. Mrs. Whitman's personal life was really none of her business.

The look of embarrassment on Elizabeth's face was hard to miss, and Annie was instantly contrite. "I'm sorry, Liz. You must think I'm a

14

real jerk, babbling on like that. You're not interested in my personal life."

"It's not that I'm not interested in you, Annie," Elizabeth protested. "It's just . . ." *It's just what?* she asked herself. *I don't want to get involved? But I'm already involved. Maybe Annie needs someone to talk to.*

"Forget it, Liz," Annie said. "Maybe we should get started on the math. You don't want to waste your whole evening on me. I'll get my books."

As Elizabeth watched Annie leave the room, she resisted the urge to shake the pretty, dark-haired girl. She sent a silent message to her sister. *Forgive me, Jess. I'm about to get in all the way.*

"Annie, let's get something straight right up front," Elizabeth said as a dejected Annie came back into the room. "You asked me for help, and I said yes. I don't think I'm wasting my time."

Annie smiled her thanks, her green eyes lighting up for a brief moment as she sat down next to Elizabeth on the sofa.

"If you've got problems you want to talk about, Annie, I'm a pretty good listener."

"Really?" Doubt was written all over Annie's face.

"Yes, really. And I've got time."

Annie got up and walked to the window, jamming her hands into the back pockets of her jeans. "Do you ever get lonely, Liz? I mean *really* lonely to talk to somebody?"

15

"Everybody gets lonely sometimes." Elizabeth tried to remember if she had ever been *really* lonely. She had her family; she had Enid Rollins, her best friend—she and Enid could talk about anything; and then there was Todd Wilkins, her boyfriend and the Gladiators' star basketball player. If only Annie had one guy like Todd, Elizabeth thought, she wouldn't need an army of other guys.

Annie turned around to face Elizabeth. There were tears in her eyes. "Liz, I don't have one real friend in the world."

As Elizabeth started to speak, Annie waved her hand. "Please, don't tell me that a mother is a girl's best friend. You don't know my mother. She's—she's different. Oh, boy, is she different!"

Annie seemed like an oil well waiting to be tapped. It all poured out—all fifteen years of a life that Elizabeth could hardly imagine.

"My mother was sixteen when I was born. Sixteen, Liz—the same age you are now! I must have been really good news for her. My father was seventeen. He married her, but they didn't live happily ever after. Are your parents together, Liz?"

The suddenness of the question startled Elizabeth. She was still trying to cope with the idea of having a baby at her age.

"Well, yes." She felt strangely guilty about having terrific parents.

Elizabeth tried to imagine what life would be like without her mother and father. Impossible, that's what! She was so proud of her tall, dark-haired, good-looking father. Even though he was one of the busiest lawyers in the area, he always had time to be with his family. What would she do without his warm support, not to mention his sense of humor?

And Mom, she thought. Did Elizabeth remember to tell her how much she appreciated everything her mother did for her? Probably not. Even with her career, Alice Wakefield was always there when the girls needed her. And it made Elizabeth so proud whenever people said that she and Jessica looked like their mother.

"My parents split up when I was two," Annie continued. "My father wasn't into responsibility, I guess."

Annie might be a year younger than she was in actual age, but Elizabeth knew she was years older in experience. "Couldn't your grandparents help?"

"Grandparents! They're the ones who are supposed to bounce you on their knees, right? Not mine. They thought my mother was *bad*—there was no way they would help."

"Annie, I'm really sorry. I had no idea." Elizabeth almost wished she hadn't said she was a good listener. This was much more than she wanted to know.

"No, Liz," Annie said, recognizing the expression on Elizabeth's face, "I don't want you to feel sorry for me. My mother's not like yours, but she's OK. She's pretty gutsy, really. She could have given me away, but she didn't. She did the best she could, I guess."

"Do you ever see your father?" Elizabeth asked, almost afraid of the answer.

Annie gave a short, bitter laugh. "He hasn't been around in five years. He used to show up once in a while—wanting money, I guess. Mom was making pretty good money modeling, and my father was out of work most of the time. He came around one day—I was about ten years old—and they had a big fight. I tried to separate them because I thought he was going to hurt Mom. He got so mad that he threw me down the stairs."

Elizabeth sat there in a state of shock. She didn't know what to say. But Annie didn't seem to need any words, only the willing ear Elizabeth had offered her.

"I did some modeling, too, a couple of years ago. Did you know that?"

Glad to be off the subject of Annie's parents, Elizabeth nodded. "I hear you were terrific at it," she said. "You've certainly got the looks for it." Even Jessica would have to admit that Annie was a knockout, with her slim figure, dark, wavy hair, and flawless complexion.

Annie laughed. "I don't know about *terrific*, Liz, but it was kind of fun for a while. I got to wear these really fabulous clothes, and people were always making a big deal about doing my makeup and fixing my hair. When they got through with me, I looked eighteen or nineteen instead of thirteen." She had a faraway look in her eyes. "Sometimes I'd look in a mirror and try to remember exactly how old I really was, you know what I mean? Everybody treated me like an adult during a modeling session, but as soon as the makeup came off and I was back in jeans, I was just a kid again."

"All that attention must have been terrific."

Annie shrugged. "Everyone said I was wonderful while the cameras were clicking, but when the session ended, they ignored me. I finally realized they didn't care about *me*, the real me beneath the makeup and the clothes. I was still lonely. My mother didn't have time for me because of her schedule, and I guess I just didn't know how to make friends with girls my own age."

"I can't imagine anyone as friendly as you are not being able to make friends, Annie."

"Well, I've got lots of boyfriends." Annie smiled brightly. "I've been deeply in love a few times. But a lot of boys are shallow, you know? Sometimes after you break up, they don't even respect you. That's what this is all about, Liz."

"What do you mean?" Elizabeth asked, still taking in everything Annie had just told her about herself.

"The grades and the cheering squad, Liz. That's the way I'm going to change my life. Don't you see? The kids will respect me if I get good grades and if I'm on something as important as the cheering squad."

"I know what you mean, Annie," Elizabeth said. "Good grades and activities *are* important, but the cheering squad isn't the only good activity. There are lots of others that are just as good." *Most of which my sister Jessica is not into,* she added to herself.

"Oh, you're wrong, Liz! There's nothing like being a cheerleader." Annie seemed amazed that anyone would put anything above the cheering squad, until she remembered whom she was talking to.

"Oh, boy, am I dumb!" Annie smacked her forehead with the heel of her hand. She was so upset she didn't see the hint of laughter in Elizabeth's eyes. "Of course. *The Oracle* is just as important. You have to be almost a genius to write the way you do!"

That did it! Elizabeth couldn't hold the amusement in. It started with a giggle. And soon, before Annie's stunned gaze, Elizabeth was doubled over with laughter.

"Oh, Annie, you're too much!" Elizabeth got out between gasps. "I don't think Mr. Collins knows he's working with a bunch of geniuses!" She knew that the faculty advisor for *The Oracle* would get at least as good a laugh out of Annie's innocent remark.

"You know what I mean, Liz," Annie said pleadingly.

"For heaven's sake, don't apologize, Annie. I know what you mean. Doing flips in front of a big crowd at a game is probably more fun than writing an article about Chrome Dome's latest set of rules, anyway," she said, remembering the dull story about the principal, Mr. Cooper, she'd gotten stuck with the week before.

Annie's eyes lit up at the thought of doing

flips in front of a big crowd. "I'm going to make it, Liz. I just know it!"

Annie was almost dancing around the room with excitement, and Elizabeth couldn't help but admire the graceful way she moved. She'd be perfect on the squad—that is, *if* Jessica gave her a chance. Those rumors about Annie just had to be exaggerated. She couldn't be as horrible as Jessica said she was. *But how do I find out the truth?* Elizabeth wondered.

"Annie, with all the schoolwork you've been doing, I guess you don't have much time for dates," Elizabeth ventured, feeling about as subtle as a Mack truck.

"Oh, sure," said Annie casually. "I think it's important to have a good social life. Actually, that's about the only good thing in my life these days. Hey, Liz, look at the time. We'd better get some work done." Annie opened her math book and binder.

Elizabeth tried to concentrate on the math problems, but at the same time she was coping with a surprising and disturbing discovery. Annie obviously had no idea of just how bad her reputation was. The poor, lonely girl saw the string of boys as her only companions. She couldn't possibly know her nickname was Easy Annie. How much was rumor and how much was fact? Elizabeth wondered.

Well, at least Annie was in a more positive mood than earlier in the evening, Elizabeth was relieved to see. *If she stays in this mood, and I can work on Jessica, just maybe we can pull it off.* Elizabeth knew she was being overoptimistic about changing her twin's mind, but it was worth a try. Annie deserved a chance to change her life, and Elizabeth was determined to help her.

An hour later, Annie stretched her arms overhead and yawned. "Wow, I'm beat, Liz, but I think I know what I'm doing. You're really great at explaining things."

"You think so?" Elizabeth hoped she would be just as great at explaining things to Jessica.

"Do you have time for a soda?"

"I really don't, but thanks, Annie." Elizabeth picked up her bag and sweater and got up to leave.

Just then the front door swung open.

"Hi, kitten, we're home," the tall, striking woman said to Annie. She flashed a dazzling smile at Elizabeth. "Hello, I'm Annie's mother."

"Hello, Mrs. Whitman. I'm Elizabeth Wakefield."

"Elizabeth! So glad to meet you," Mrs. Whitman gushed, her words slightly slurred from drinking.

"Mom, Liz has to leave," Annie cut in anxiously. "She came over to help me with math. Thanks a lot, Liz," she said, half pushing Elizabeth toward the door. The happy, confident mood of a few minutes earlier had vanished.

"Aren't you going to introduce me to your pretty little tutor, kid?" The man lounging in the open doorway leered at Elizabeth, making her skin crawl. Annie was rigid with anger.

"*This* is Johnny," Annie said through clenched teeth.

"Hello, Mr.—?" Elizabeth wished she had left five minutes earlier.

"Just call me Johnny, sugar. All the cute little girls call me Johnny."

"Johnny, I said Liz had to leave," Annie said, pushing him aside and walking Elizabeth to the elevator.

"Liz, I don't know what to say." Annie scuffed the toe of her shoe back and forth on the hall carpet as they stood waiting for the elevator.

"Annie, you don't have to say anything."

"What's the use of kidding myself, Liz? Nothing ever works out the way I want it to."

"You've got to believe in yourself, Annie!" Elizabeth insisted. "Hey, I believe in you. Could a genius like me make a mistake?" That almost brought a smile to Annie's face.

Riding the bus home, Elizabeth reflected on the situation. It was easy enough to encourage Annie, but trying to manipulate Jessica would be something entirely different. "OK, genius," she muttered, "think of something."

Three

Jessica was in her element. On the patio at the rear of the Wakefield house, she was drilling Cara Walker on every move she'd need to know to become a member of the Sweet Valley cheering squad once again.

"All you have to learn are some new cheers, and the fancy moves we've added since you were there," Jessica explained. "And of course you know all about following the captain."

She meant herself, of course. Robin Wilson was co-captain, but she didn't really spend as much time on the squad as Jessica. So the girls looked to Jessica for leadership, which was exactly the way it should be, Jessica felt.

Cara looked exhausted from the workout she was getting. Sweat poured down her face, and her breath was coming in gasps. "Jessica, practice never used to be this tough," Cara wailed. "What do you think I am, an Olympic athlete?"

"You're doing fine," Jessica assured her. "Just work on that split a little."

Cara stretched her tanned legs forward and backward, feeling muscles tighten and tendons strain.

Jessica was satisfied. With her personal coaching, Cara was sure to get back on the squad with no trouble.

"Are you pretty sure I'll make it?" Cara asked from her torturous split beside the Wakefield pool. "I mean, I'd die of embarrassment if my old teammates didn't think I was good enough anymore."

"I guarantee it," Jessica said.

Cara smiled. "It'll be good to be back. Who else is going to be chosen?"

"Well, I'm not sure," said Jessica. "How do you like Sandra Bacon?"

"Oh, she's all right," Cara said. "Not always the most graceful, though. Remember the time—"

"At Lila's pool party," Jessica finished, breaking into a delighted giggle.

"Could you believe how she was showing off up there on the diving board? Like she was about to execute a triple-flip swan dive or something." Cara lifted herself out of her split.

"And Mark wasn't paying the teeniest bit of attention to her." Jessica snorted. "Until she fell off the edge of the board and into the water on her belly."

Cara doubled over, holding her stomach in helpless laughter, tears pouring from her eyes at the memory. She heard Jessica clearing her throat and wondered if she had gone too far. After all, Jessica *had* suggested Sandra for the cheering squad. But then Cara saw the large blue sneaker in front of her face. She looked up. There stood Steven Wakefield, the twins' brother. Cara felt her cheeks turn crimson. Steven Wakefield, the boy she'd had a terrific crush on for years and years, was standing there, and she was groveling around on the patio like a snake!

Cara immediately rolled around and sat up.

"Hi, Steve," she murmured, blushing to the roots of her hair.

Steven didn't seem upset by her contortions, Cara decided. She looked more closely and decided he hardly even seemed to know she was there.

"Hi, Steve," Jessica was saying. "What brings you home from college?"

"Huh?" said Steven.

"Cara's going to be back on the cheering squad," Jessica said. "Isn't that great?"

"What?" Steven said, glancing around at Cara. "Oh, sure. I guess so." He hurried into the house.

Jessica frowned. Cara would be just right for Steven, if he would only wake up and stop mooning over Tricia Martin. The whole Martin family was nothing but trouble, the trashiest people in Sweet Valley, and Steven had to be mixed up with them. Elizabeth was constantly telling her that Tricia was a special person, but

26

Jessica knew that one Martin was as bad as another.

"I guess I messed that up, all right," Cara was saying. "Boy! He must think I'm some idiot!"

"He does not," Jessica declared. "He's just—preoccupied. Sooner or later I'll get the two of you together. Just you wait."

Cara glanced toward the house, where Steven had disappeared. She sighed. "Well, I've got to be going. See you at the tryouts." She gathered up her books.

"OK," said Jessica. "And don't worry. It's in the bag."

As Cara disappeared around the side of the house, Jessica hurried inside. She knew that look on her brother's face spelled trouble. She found him in the kitchen, reaching for the telephone.

"What happened?" she inquired.

Steven looked grim. "An accident."

Jessica's heart leaped into her mouth. "What? What kind of accident?"

"Tricia's father," Steven said. "He hit a woman on Palmetto Drive."

"Oh, no!" Jessica cried.

"I've got to call Tricia," Steven said. "She must be really upset."

"Is the woman hurt badly?"

Steven shook his head. "I don't think so, but I don't know for sure. I found out about the accident from a friend of Tricia's. I *do* know that Mr. Martin's in jail for a few days."

"Jail?" Jessica gasped, horrified.

"He was busted for drunk driving again."

Jessica sank down onto a chair, furious that the Wakefields were in any way associated with the revolting Martin family.

"Oh, Steve," she said, "I told you the Martins were all rotten. For Pete's sake, why don't you let me fix you up with Cara? She's terrific!"

"Knock it off, Jess," Steven said. "Tricia needs me. I've got to get over there." He anxiously began dialing the phone.

Jessica stomped out of the kitchen, feeling only helplessness at her brother's infatuation with Tricia. She couldn't get over the feeling that one day her brother would come to grief because of his love for that girl.

The gym at Sweet Valley High looked like backstage at a Broadway musical casting call as the seventy-five hopefuls showed up for cheerleader tryouts the next afternoon. It was sheer bedlam, girls everywhere dashing around trying cartwheels and cheers, squealing as they greeted each other.

"Wow!" Robin Wilson was wide-eyed. "How are we going to handle this mob?"

"Can you belive it," said Helen Bradley, the bubbly redhead. "You'd think we were giving away Mr. America."

Jessica climbed onto a bench, stuck her whistle in her mouth, and issued a screeching blast. "Attention, everybody," she yelled.

It took a couple more whistle blasts, but finally the crowd quieted down and focused their attention on Jessica.

"I'm Jessica Wakefield, in case anybody doesn't know, and this is Robin Wilson. We're co-captains. This is Helen Bradley and Jean West and Maria Santelli."

The cheerleaders got a nice round of applause, which pleased Jessica. She was happy to see a good turnout of students up in the stands, too, including Helen Bradley's good-looking brother, Tim.

Elizabeth was also there, taking notes for an *Oracle* story. With her was Enid Rollins.

"I know why you're here." Enid fixed her lovely green eyes on Elizabeth. "To write a story. But why am I here? I know you didn't drag me along to hear who I think does the best splits."

"Quiet, slave," Elizabeth teased. "You're here because I need somebody who can talk about something other than cheerleading."

Back on the floor, Jessica continued her introductions. "Now, girls," she said, "I want you to meet the person we all depend upon, the brains of the organization, the heart and the soul of the squad, and please don't rip his clothes off."

The other cheerleaders were all giggling, knowing what was coming.

"Here he is," said Jessica. "Our manager— Ricky Capaldo."

Ricky Capaldo, his face red as a fire engine, came trotting out from under the stands, giving Jessica a murderous look. Ricky was small and dark and shy, and not what anyone would call handsome. But those who looked closely were sure to notice his warm brown eyes. He put up with a lot of teasing, but all of it was friendly. Even Jessica was fond of him. Ricky carried a clipboard with several sheets of paper on it, a list of all the names of the girls trying out. In a few minutes, he got the girls separated into five groups spread out across the gym.

Jessica's silver whistle blasted again.

"OK, everybody, today's tryout is to pick twenty-five semifinalists. We can already see that it's going to be tough—after all, Sweet Valley High has the most talented and beautiful girls in California."

That got a loud cheer.

"Good luck!" Jessica shouted.

Ricky Capaldo moved swiftly up and down the gym, handing out scoring sheets to Jessica, Robin, Helen, Jean, and Maria. The five members of the squad stood in front of the five groups, showing them the routines and calling out the cheers.

Jessica was in front of the group that included the last part of the alphabet. She saw Cara Walker and winked. Then another face came into her vision, a smiling, eager, beautiful face. Annie Whitman. Jessica turned away. *She really had the nerve to show up!*

Each girl came forward as her name was called and did the basic Gladiator cheer, the side kicks, the Y-leap, and the final flourish, yelling: "We who are about to win, salute you! Go, Gladiators!"

It didn't take long for the members of the squad to see that the seventy-five aspirants could easily be reduced to about forty. There were the freshmen, who almost never got on the squad, and knew they were practicing for their sophomore year. Then there were the ones who couldn't get off the ground, or tripped and went sprawling, or got stage fright and ran out of the gym.

Cara Walker sailed through the first cheer as if she'd never left the team. Jessica was congratulating herself on coaching her friend when Annie Whitman stepped forward and began her routine.

All that was required for the first routine was a simple cheer, but Annie performed with a grace that made the cheer extra special. She added flourishes and fancy moves that some of the girls on the squad had been working on for months.

"Go, Gladiators!" Annie yelled, leaping through every motion with precision and ease. It was apparent to everyone watching, except perhaps Jessica, that Annie was quite simply the most talented new girl there, and one of the prettiest as well. She finished off by dashing across the floor into two cartwheels and sailing high into a final, breathtaking back flip that made even Maria Santelli proud.

Applause exploded in the gym. Annie, her face flushed with excitement and happiness, returned to her place among the hopefuls, who heaped congratulations upon her. Jessica's face

31

was possibly the only one in the gym that wasn't happy.

The glow of Annie's triumph was still floating in the air when Sandra Bacon jogged to the center of the gym with her group and stepped out to take her turn. Jessica watched her hopefully and was pleased to see Sandy move quite satisfactorily through the cheer.

Ricky Capaldo circulated among the five cheerleaders, collecting the sheets with their choices for the twenty-five semifinalists. Passing Annie, he gave her a broad and encouraging smile.

"Great going, Miss Flashdance," he joked.

Annie blushed prettily.

Ricky made his way through the crowd of eager girls, seated himself on a bench, and began tallying the votes. Cara Walker was in, as was Sandra Bacon, and, of course, Annie Whitman.

"Hey, Jess," said Ricky, "you forgot to put Annie's name on your sheet."

"Who?" said Jessica.

"Annie Whitman. Everybody put her name down. You must have forgotten."

"I didn't forget, Ricky," said Jessica.

Just then, Annie came running up to them, glowing and happy.

"Is that all for today?" she said. "Because I have a date."

I'll bet you have, Jessica thought angrily.

"Yep, that's it," Ricky said warmly. "The list will be posted tomorrow."

32

Annie flashed a smile at Jessica, then hurried back toward the stands.

Jessica watched her in annoyance. She saw Annie move up the steps to join handsome Tim Bradley.

"But he's a senior, and she's only a sophomore," Jessica muttered. She was mildly interested in Tim herself and had thought he was there to watch her and maybe to buy her a Coke afterward. But there he was, leaving with Easy Annie!

She turned to see Helen sitting beside her, checking the selections.

"You'd better keep an eye on your brother, Helen," Jessica hissed.

"What?" Helen said, looking toward the stands. Tim and Annie were standing close together.

"Do you see who he's with?"

"Annie Whitman?"

"Don't you care if your brother runs around with the school tramp?" Jessica snapped.

Helen Bradley frowned unhappily as she watched Tim and Annie leaving the gym together. "I have heard the rumors," she said.

"They aren't rumors," Jessica said, and to herself she made a vow: *Easy Annie will never be on the cheerleading squad, and that's final!*

While Jessica watched Tim and Annie, someone had her eye on Jessica. And that someone had a pretty good idea of what was going through Jessica's head. *She's really got it in for Annie*, Elizabeth thought. *And I can't think of a single way to change her mind.*

"I want you to know it's been really fantastic talking with you, Liz," Enid joked lightly.

Elizabeth continued staring at Jessica in silence.

"I mean, I'm so glad you brought me along to keep you company."

Still there was no response from Elizabeth.

"Hey! Earth to Wakefield. Come in, Wakefield." Enid practically shouted, giving Elizabeth a gentle poke in the ribs. "Liz, what *is* the matter? Watching tryouts is supposed to be fun."

"Everything's fine, Enid." Elizabeth forced a small smile. "I mean, I *am* having fun. Especially watching Annie Whitman. She's terrific, isn't she?"

"Yeah, terrific, Liz, so why that very *un*terrific look on your face?"

"What look?" Elizabeth asked a little too sharply.

"Like you just saw something black and creepy crawl across the floor or maybe overheard a plot to destroy the world—that look."

Elizabeth giggled. "You're a nut, Enid Rollins."

"That's me all right, old Zany Rollins," Enid said dryly. "Seriously, Liz, you look upset. And you were watching Jessica, not Annie. What's your sister up to this time?"

Enid was all too familiar with Jessica's schemes, having been the target of one of them not too long ago. She wouldn't trust Jessica Wakefield as far as she could throw a truck.

34

"Oh, you know Jess—always up to something," Elizabeth joked. But inside she was worried. Once Jessica had made up her mind, there was nothing anyone could do to change it.

Four

Ricky Capaldo had never in his life felt so popular and so disliked at one instant. Word spread almost before he had the first thumbtack into the bulletin board in front of the girls' gym. He was immediately engulfed by half the females at Sweet Valley High, pushing and yelling as they fought to see which names were on the list. To those hopefuls who had been cut, Ricky became the object of intense outrage. But the twenty-five who made it were bouncing with joy, several of them hugging and kissing the shy, blushing squad manager.

"Hey, I don't even get to vote," Ricky protested, to no avail.

Elizabeth was making her way down the corridor in time to see Ricky surrounded by the happy girls. Annie Whitman's arms were around his neck, and she gave him a kiss.

"I think I'll post a list every day," Ricky said, laughing.

Turning around, Annie spotted Elizabeth and immediately ran over to give her a hug, too.

"Liz, I made it," Annie squealed. "Isn't it wonderful?"

Elizabeth laughed happily. "Yes, it sure is."

"I've still got to make the other cuts, though," said Annie, falling in step with Elizabeth. "Do you think you could possibly help me again? We've got a monster test coming up."

"Sure," Elizabeth answered. "Just say when."

"Well, let's see," Annie said, apparently doing a mental run-through of her busy schedule. "Tonight—no, I have a date tonight."

"Don't forget that I'm the 'Eyes and Ears' of Sweet Valley High," Elizabeth said. "Can I write that you and Tim Bradley are an item?"

"Tim Bradley?" Annie said casually. "Oh, I saw him once, but I'm not really interested."

Elizabeth marveled at the swiftness of Annie Whitman's romances. She had thought Tim was the very latest of Annie's boyfriends.

"Who then?" Elizabeth asked teasingly. "Ricky?"

Annie turned an astonished face upon Elizabeth. "Ricky Capaldo?" she said, wide-eyed.

"Well, the way you kissed him back there . . ."

Annie giggled. "I was just carried away! I never thought of Ricky as a boyfriend, you know? He always seems like—I don't know, just a pal."

Elizabeth nodded slowly. Most of the girls liked Ricky a lot, but as sort of a buddy.

"Well, then, who's the lucky guy?" Elizabeth was almost afraid to find out.

Annie smiled mysteriously. "Promise not to tell?"

"Remember, I'm a reporter," Elizabeth teased again.

Annie blushed. "OK, but don't let anybody know where you got this. I've got a date with Billy and Rick."

"Huh?"

Annie laughed and her eyes danced. "Billy's taking me to the Dairi Burger, and then later on Rick Andover is taking me to the beach for a late swim."

Elizabeth studied Annie in amazement. Here was a girl fighting to keep her grades up so she could make the cheering squad, but she had two dates. She already had a bad reputation but was perfectly willing to have an item in *The Oracle* about her going out with two guys, one of them a dropout with a really bad name around town.

"Annie," said Elizabeth, "you're a wonder."

Annie smiled, taking it as a compliment. "Boys I can handle. It's math that's a pain in the neck."

Annie waved and walked off down the corridor. "We'll set something up later, OK?"

"Fine," Elizabeth called after her.

Elizabeth didn't print the item about Annie's "double-date." Instead, she put in the names of the girls who had made the first cut on the cheering squad and mentioned that Annie Whitman, Cara Walker, and Sandy Bacon looked like the favorites.

The story in *The Oracle* had seemed to Elizabeth a fairly ordinary item, until she was pounced upon a few days later by a furious Jessica.

"Elizabeth Wakefield," Jessica declared as they were getting ready for school, "aren't there any rules in journalism about printing the truth?"

"Pardon me?" Elizabeth said, tuning in to her twin sister's building anger.

"What do you mean by saying that Easy Annie is one of the favorites to make the cheerleading squad?"

"Jess, everybody thought she was terrific."

"Not everybody! Not some of the more important members of the squad."

"OK. So you don't like her. Did you hear the applause she got?"

"Sure," said Jessica. "All her boyfriends. That's about two hundred right there. And I'm not the only one. Helen Bradley is on to her now, too."

"Uh-oh," said Elizabeth. "Did Tim Bradley tell her something?"

"Only everything. That Easy Annie lived up to her nickname all the way, that's all." Jessica rummaged through her twin's closet until she found the blouse she was looking for.

"I'm sorry, Jess," Elizabeth said. "But I report what I see, and Annie was the most popular girl to·try out. Those are facts."

"Yes, and she'll never make the squad. That's another fact," Jessica snapped.

"How do you know that?"

"Because I know."

Jessica disappeared into the bathroom, slamming the door before Elizabeth could question her further. *Maybe Annie will get so interested in some guy that she'll forget about cheerleading,* Elizabeth thought. *Sure, and maybe the Pacific Ocean will dry up and become a desert,* she added to herself.

Elizabeth was on the front lawn one afternoon when Annie dashed up to her, hugged her, and said, "I got an A on the math test! I think I'll nominate you for Woman of the Year!"

Despite her many dates, Annie seemed to have gotten the hang of math. Elizabeth had gone to Annie's apartment two more times to coach her, each time hiding her visit from Jessica.

She thought back to the last session and sighed out loud. She and Annie had just taken out their books when the doorbell rang. Annie got up to open the door, and Elizabeth could see a tiny gray-haired woman standing in the hallway.

"Annie, dear," the old lady said timidly, "I'm afraid I've misplaced my glasses, again."

"Don't worry, Mrs. Jorgenson." Annie put her arm around the woman's shoulder and gave her a gentle squeeze. "I always find them for you, don't I?" Annie turned back to Elizabeth. "I shouldn't be more than a few minutes. Would you mind waiting?" she asked apologetically.

Elizabeth smiled. "Go ahead. Of course I'll wait. I've got some work of my own to look at while you're on the great hunt."

A minute after Annie dashed out to Mrs.

Jorgenson's rescue, Elizabeth heard a key turn in the lock. *Oh, no,* she thought. *Just what I need, a chat with Mrs. Whitman and call-me-Johnny.* She had managed to avoid being alone with them since the first tutoring session. They both made her nervous.

"Hi, kitten, I'm home!" Mrs. Whitman called out as she whirled into the room. Seeing Elizabeth sitting on the white sofa, Mrs. Whitman flashed her a brilliant smile. "Hi, um . . ." A frown crossed her face. "Now don't tell me. I know you. You're—ah, you're—"

"Elizabeth Wakefield, Mrs. Whitman." Thank goodness Johnny wasn't with her, Elizabeth thought.

There was another brilliant smile. "Of course. Annie's pretty friend with the pretty name."

Hurry back, Annie, please, Elizabeth prayed to herself.

"Where's my baby?" Mrs. Whitman asked.

Relieved to be off the subject of her pretty name, Elizabeth told her that Annie had gone down the hall to help out a neighbor.

"Oh, I bet it's that loony old Mrs. Jorgenson," Mrs. Whitman said in disgust. "Why Annie lets that old lady bother her is beyond me. She'd be better off staying here with a nice friend like you. And I'm going to tell her how rude she's being," Mrs. Whitman concluded. The smell of liquor mixed with the scent of her perfume.

"No, it's all right, Mrs. Whitman. Really it is," Elizabeth protested. "I think it's nice of

Annie to help out like that." *You could probably learn something from your daughter*, she added silently.

"Well, of course," said Mrs. Whitman, changing her viewpoint at once. "That's my Annie. She's so sweet, so generous with her time. I've always encouraged her to be kind to everyone."

I'll bet you have, Elizabeth thought as she watched Mrs. Whitman sink gracefully into a dark blue, velour-covered chair. The blue was a perfect backdrop for Mrs. Whitman's white slacks and long-sleeved, white silk shirt. No one could deny that she had the looks and poise of a professional model.

"Tell me about you and Annie, Elizabeth. Have you been good friends a long time?" The bright smile was back on her lips.

Elizabeth winced at being put on the spot like that.

"Well, Mrs. Whitman, Annie and I have *known* each other for about a year. I like Annie, but I don't know if you could say we're really good friends."

As she saw the disappointed look on Mrs. Whitman's face, Elizabeth quickly added, "Annie's a year younger than I am, you know. I'm sure her *good* friends are girls her own age."

Mrs. Whitman didn't respond for a few minutes. "I guess you're right," she said slowly. "I hope you're right, Elizabeth. I've just never met any of them." There was a long, awkward pause.

Finally Mrs. Whitman spoke again. "Elizabeth, may I talk to you about Annie?"

Wishing she could say no, Elizabeth said, "Sure."

"Is my little girl, ah . . . well liked at school?"

"Well liked?" Elizabeth echoed.

"I mean, is she popular?"

Oh, boy, Elizabeth thought. *Popular doesn't say half of it.* Elizabeth wondered if Mrs. Whitman took any notice at all of her daughter's comings and goings. She appeared to be genuinely concerned about Annie, but she didn't seem to understand how important it was to make the time to pay attention to her. She was simply too wrapped up in her own doings.

"I'm probably not the right person to ask, Mrs. Whitman," Elizabeth hedged, "but from what I've seen, I think Annie's popular."

Mrs. Whitman let out her breath in relief. "I'm so glad to hear that. I worry about my baby. You see, my schedule keeps me so busy that I don't have much time for Annie."

My mother's busy, too, Elizabeth wanted to say. *But she always has time for Jessica and me.*

"And of course there's Johnny."

Elizabeth shivered at the mention of his name.

"I just wish Annie would bring more of her friends home," Mrs. Whitman continued. "She should have parties at home, like the other kids do. Don't you agree, Elizabeth?"

"Well, I think that's up to Annie, Mrs. Whitman." Elizabeth knew that if she were Annie,

43

she wouldn't want to invite her friends to this home.

Annie burst through the door. "You'll never guess where I found her glasses this time! They were on the pantry shelf between the cat food and the plastic—" The smile left her face, and the light seemed to go out of her eyes as she looked from her mother to Elizabeth.

"Mom," she said, "how long have you been home?"

"Just a few minutes, baby," Mrs. Whitman said, getting to her feet. "I'll leave you two pretty girls to get on with your work. It was nice to see you again, Elizabeth," she said as she left the room.

" 'Bye, Mrs. Whitman," Elizabeth called to the retreating back.

Annie looked at Elizabeth nervously. "What was my mother saying to you?" she asked, a note of fear in her voice.

Elizabeth crossed her fingers behind her back. "Oh, we were talking about school and things," she fibbed.

But the study sessions had been worth it. Annie had sailed through a small quiz, and now she'd passed the really big test, the one that decided the grade for the marking period.

"Annie, I'm so proud of you." Elizabeth was glowing. "This is even bigger news than the cheerleader tryouts."

Annie grew sober, and she stared at Elizabeth. "Oh, Liz, don't even say that. Nothing else will count if I don't make the squad."

Walking home that day, Elizabeth wondered why she had done it again. Why had she gotten involved in Annie Whitman's life when she knew perfectly well that Jessica hated the girl? Maybe that was the reason. Because poor Annie just didn't realize what a powerful enemy she had.

Elizabeth sighed, resolving to forget about the whole problem and concentrate on the evening ahead. The round of tests that had kept everyone studying was now over. That meant a full house at the Beach Disco that night. Elizabeth couldn't wait to let loose with Todd on the dance floor.

The crowd was already going strong by the time they arrived that night. The Surfers' Waves, a band from Northern California, were playing some hot new tunes, and everybody was having a terrific time. Jessica was there with Skip Harmon. She was wearing a black-and-red striped top and her shortest skirt. It had taken her almost two weeks to get Skip to ask her out, because Skip was a senior and had often told everyone he never looked at any of the junior girls.

"He'll look at me," Jessica had told Elizabeth. "And what's more, he'll ask me out within a week."

Elizabeth had laughed. "No way."

"What do we bet?"

"Who washes the Fiat next?"

"You're on," Jessica said.

Dancing with Todd, Elizabeth made a mental

note never to bet against Jessica when it came to snagging a guy.

"Want to help me wash the car Saturday?" she said in Todd's ear.

"Sure," he answered. "I'll help you do anything." He drew her closer.

She smiled. "Easy, caveman."

Yes, it was shaping up as a wonderful, relaxing evening until Elizabeth happened to notice that Jessica had stopped dancing with Skip and was staring fixedly across the floor.

Elizabeth followed her sister's gaze. Annie Whitman was walking through the door—instantly catching everybody's attention in a slinky outfit with a skirt that had a slit almost to the top of her thigh. And as if that wasn't enough, she was accompanied by none other than Bruce Patman, the handsome, arrogant captain of the Sweet Valley High tennis team and the son of one of the wealthiest men in town.

Bruce was also Jessica's number-one deadly enemy. For the briefest time they had been the golden couple of the school, but their relationship had turned into a battle of wits that Jessica wasn't likely to forget. And now, any iota of a chance that Annie Whitman might have had with Jessica was blown to smithereens as she and Bruce made their way toward the dance floor.

Elizabeth sighed and shook her head. The wonderful, relaxing evening was starting to slide downhill.

Picking up on her mood instantly, as he always seemed to do, Todd leaned his face toward hers and looked into her eyes. "What's the matter, Liz? Are you feeling all right?"

"Hmmm?"

He gave her a gentle hug. " 'Hmmm' isn't much of an answer. What's up?"

Elizabeth sighed again before answering. "I'm sorry, Todd." She squeezed his hand in apology. "I suddenly wish we were someplace else."

"You want me to carry you out of this place," he offered, bending as if to lift her into his arms. "Me Tarzan, you Jane. Let's go find a couple of vines."

His grin was irresistible. Laughing, she punched him lightly in the midsection. "You idiot, me worrier. And vines are my least favorite form of transportation."

"What *is* my favorite worrier worrying about this evening?" Todd asked tenderly.

Just as Elizabeth was about to pour her heart out, Todd suddenly smacked his forehead with the back of his hand.

"Why am I even asking?" he said, his voice rising. "They don't call us dumb jocks for nothing. It's Jessica, isn't it?" he demanded. "Jess is in some kind of trouble—or about to be—and you're going to bail her out *again*."

"That's not fair, Todd. I know Jessica's not your favorite person in the world, but she is my twin. You could try giving her the benefit of the doubt every once in a while." Todd's dislike for Jessica was a sore spot for Elizabeth. Trouble though she might be, no one attacked Jessica and got away with it when Elizabeth was around. Not even Todd.

Todd faced Elizabeth and shook his head. "I'm sorry," he said. "I didn't mean to upset you. I just want to help. Like I said, jocks are dumb."

Elizabeth looked up at him. Tall and lean, with warm brown eyes, Todd looked especially handsome that night in his gray cords and burgundy shirt. Why did he put up with her? She always seemed to take out her frustration about Jessica on him.

"I don't think jocks are dumb," she said quietly. "I think you're the smartest basketball player I've ever dated." She moved a step closer to him.

"How many have you dated?" he asked.

"Only one."

"Good," he said, pulling her close to him.

Jessica was still eyeing Annie when the Beach Disco's manager, a heavyset man named Mel, jumped up on the bandstand and announced a dance contest. The Surfers' Waves began whipping up a foam of music, and Todd and Elizabeth happily plunged into the rhythm, along with Jessica and Skip Harmon, and Annie Whitman and Bruce Patman.

There were plenty of good dancers at the Beach Disco that night, but it didn't take long to see that Skip Harmon was the best dancer of all the guys on the floor. He and Jessica whirled around the Beach Disco, outclassing everybody.

Except for one other couple.

Though Bruce Patman wasn't quite as smooth a dancer as Skip, he was pretty flashy and had a lot of style. But what made Bruce look particularly good was his partner—Annie Whitman.

Annie, it was clear to see, was a natural.

Mel danced around holding his hand over the heads of the couples to see who got the most applause, and finally only two couples were left on the floor—Skip Harmon and Jessica, and Annie and Bruce.

All the kids at Sweet Valley knew that Jessica was one of the best dancers at school. Her blond hair streamed out around her as she moved in perfect harmony with the music. But nobody had ever seen Annie Whitman on the dance floor before. It was clear that Jessica had some stiff competition.

Mel held his hand over the heads of Jessica and Skip, then over Annie and Bruce. He continued to run back and forth as the disco rocked with applause that was just as loud for one couple as for the other.

Finally Mel gave an exaggerated shrug of helplessness. Then he grabbed Jessica's hand and held it up and grabbed Annie's hand and held it up, too, to indicate a draw.

Annie turned toward Jessica, a look of absolute happiness on her face.

"You and me, Jess—isn't it great!"

Jessica's plastered-on smile didn't waver, but Elizabeth saw that look and knew it was carved out of purest ice.

Later on, Elizabeth ran into Annie as they

were all leaving. Annie was still bubbling with triumph.

"Wasn't that something?" she said, laughing.

"It sure was," Elizabeth said.

"I showed Jessica I was good, didn't I?"

Elizabeth smiled. "Yes, you did." But she was thinking, *You didn't just show her—you showed her up!*

"Don't you think this will make a difference?" Annie asked.

Oh, yes, it'll make a difference, Elizabeth thought. The odds against Annie's making the cheerleading squad had just gone up to about a million to one.

Five

How could the same event cause exactly the opposite reactions in two different people? Elizabeth wondered. And yet that's what had happened. Annie Whitman thought that by showing Jessica she could dance just as well as Jessica could, it meant her selection as a cheerleader was now certain.

And Jessica made it clear to Elizabeth that Annie's "disgustingly showy performance" at the Beach Disco meant she would *never* be a cheerleader.

As they walked to school Monday morning, Elizabeth sighed. She had been listening to Jessica ranting all weekend. "Jess, exactly what is it that you think she did?"

"What? Why, she made a total fool of herself in front of everybody," Jessica snapped.

"By dancing?"

"By dancing with Bruce Patman!"

Elizabeth examined her sister's angry face.

"Jess, is it just possible that you're so angry because Annie did as well as you did?"

"That's absurd," Jessica raged. "Besides, she *wasn't* as good. It was just the novelty of seeing her dance for the first time. Everybody was surprised."

"You're wrong," Elizabeth said. "Annie's a terrific dancer."

"The nerve, the absolute nerve of her standing there trying to pretend she's as good as I am," Jessica howled. "As good as you or any of us."

"Well, isn't she?"

"No! Double no. Triple no! A thousand times no! You want to say Easy Annie is acceptable? No, no, no, no, no!"

The twins were almost in front of Sweet Valley High as the discussion heated up. It was the day of the cheerleading semifinals, and Elizabeth knew it was a critical day for Annie. But all Elizabeth's attempts at softening Jessica's attitude toward Annie had failed. It looked more hopeless than ever.

"Maybe she'll flunk the marking period," Jessica said hopefully. "Maybe they'll put her back on probation, and she won't be eligible."

"I don't think she'll fail," Elizabeth said.

"I just don't understand it," Jessica complained. "How did she get so smart lately? She used to be so stupid."

"Jess, I really think she's trying to change for the better. She's been studying and working hard. And making the cheerleading squad is

52

about the most important thing in her life right now. It would do her a world of good."

"How do you know she's been studying? Why, she's out with a different guy every night! Bruce Patman, Rick Andover, and Lord knows who else."

Elizabeth walked on in silence. It was true. Annie kept right on dating, keeping her "popularity" up, as she put it.

Jessica was still fuming as they neared the wide green lawns of the high school. "Did it ever occur to you, Liz, that letting her on the squad would do us all a world of harm?"

"Not if she's changing, Jess!"

"Well, she isn't! She's still Easy Annie."

Jessica left her sister on the front steps and marched off defiantly. As she hurried along to her locker, she felt certain that she'd be able to cut Annie Whitman at the semifinals that afternoon. The first time, Annie had been amazingly lucky. But could she repeat her performance? Jessica wondered. With all the studying she must have been doing recently, not to mention all the dating, she couldn't possibly have had time to practice her cheers. Jessica was confident that Annie wouldn't be prepared.

The second cut would reduce the number of would-be cheerleaders from twenty-five to eight. Cara Walker and Sandra Bacon were going to be among that eight, Jessica had decided, and Annie Whitman was definitely not going to be.

She wasn't prejudging Annie, Jessica told

herself. It was just that she knew the girl would fall on her face.

Later in the day, Elizabeth sat in the *Oracle* office, typing her latest "Eyes and Ears" column and congratulating herself on having helped Annie with her studying while still escaping detection. In other words, Jessica hadn't found out, which was a great relief. She was putting the finishing touches on the column when Jessica herself walked into the office with a list of the eight finalists.

"Already?" asked a surprised Elizabeth. "I thought the tryouts weren't until after school."

"Well, they aren't," Jessica confessed, "but you won't make your deadline if we wait till then. You can be sure this is the list."

Elizabeth scanned the names.

"Jessica!" she scolded.

Jessica Wakefield's eyes widened—pure innocence personified. "I'm trying to give you a scoop, Liz."

"I'll take the list—*after* the tryouts."

And then who should dash into the *Oracle* office but Annie Whitman, all aglow.

"I made it," she gushed to Jessica. "A B-minus in math! Oh, Liz, how can I ever thank you enough for helping me?"

Annie gave Elizabeth a huge hug before dashing back out of the office and off to her next class. "See you at the gym!" she told Jessica as she was leaving.

"*So!*" declared Jessica as soon as Annie had disappeared.

Elizabeth turned toward her work.

"Traitor!"

Elizabeth typed furiously.

"I knew somebody was helping that girl," Jessica fumed, "but I never dreamed it would be my very own flesh and blood!"

Elizabeth stopped and looked pleadingly at her twin. "Give her a chance, Jess, will you?"

Jessica's answer was to turn and march out of the room.

Elizabeth lifted her fingers from the keyboard and rested her chin on her hand. "What timing," she muttered. "Why couldn't one of them have come in five minutes later?"

"Is this a private conversation, or can a mere teacher get in on it?" The words, accompanied by a soft chuckle, startled Elizabeth.

"What?" she said, turning quickly to see Mr. Collins in the doorway. The good-looking *Oracle* adviser was grinning at her.

If another teacher had caught her talking to herself, Elizabeth might have been embarrassed. But Mr. Collins was different. Every girl in Sweet Valley High knew just how different Roger Collins was. In his late twenties, he was one of the youngest teachers on the faculty. Everything about him—his tall, slim build, his strawberry-blond hair, the well-cut sport jackets he wore—seemed perfect. "He makes the rest of the teachers look like they shop at the Salvation Army," Jessica had once said.

But what made Roger Collins really popular with the kids at Sweet Valley—the guys as well

55

as the girls—was the way he looked at things. Maybe it was because of his age, but he could always be counted on to see the kids' side of things.

Mr. Collins walked across the room to where Elizabeth was sitting. "What's got my star reporter talking to herself?" he asked, still smiling at her. "Do you want to talk to me about it?"

"I think I do. I *know* I do. But I don't know if I should." Elizabeth stared down at the typewriter keys in indecision. She could really use Mr. Collins's advice, but if she told him what was going on with Annie and Jessica, it would put her sister in an awful light. Not only would that be disloyal, but Jessica would probably never forgive her if she found out—and Jessica seemed to have a way of always finding out.

"Maybe you should sign up for that new course being offered next year," Mr. Collins suggested lightly.

"Excuse me?" Elizabeth looked at him in confusion.

"The course is called Decisions, something you seem to have a little trouble with at the moment."

"I think I'd better be first in line," Elizabeth said, breaking into a small smile. "You see, Mr. Collins, this problem I have is—is not really my problem, but I've gotten kind of involved, somehow. . . ." Her voice trailed off.

"That's what I like in a reporter, Wakefield. Clear, concise, to the point."

Elizabeth responded to Mr. Collins's teasing

with a giggle. He knew just how to make a person relax, Elizabeth thought. It was so easy to open up and talk to him.

"I'm trying to help someone get something she really wants, something really good for her," Elizabeth began. "But there's someone else who doesn't want her to have this good thing. And this someone else has what she thinks are good reasons." Elizabeth looked up at him, appealing for a solution.

"And you're stuck in the middle, right?" Mr. Collins said.

"I sure am."

"And both girls are good friends of yours," he continued.

Was Annie a good friend? Elizabeth hadn't really thought about it that way before. But Mr. Collins was right. Annie had become a friend. And Jessica was her twin, the person closest to her in the whole world. That made her even more than a friend.

"Yes, they're both people I care about. And I'm just afraid one of them is going to get hurt." Elizabeth looked toward Mr. Collins, who nodded encouragingly.

"And what about you?" he asked, pulling up a chair and sitting down. "You could end up hurt, too, if you get involved in their problems."

Elizabeth thought about how much Annie was depending on her for support and how little she could really do. Then she pictured Jessica's angry face of a few minutes ago. She was liable to wind up disappointing both of them if she wasn't careful.

"I guess the most I can do is to be a good friend to both of them and let them work out their differences for themselves, right?" Elizabeth leaned back in her chair and studied Mr. Collins for confirmation.

"It's not for nothing that you're my star reporter, Wakefield." He tousled her hair playfully.

"Thanks for listening, Mr. Collins." For the first time all day, the cheering tryouts didn't seem to Elizabeth like the beginning and end of the world.

But they did seem that way to Annie, Cara, Sandra, and all the rest of the squad hopefuls. They met that afternoon in the gym, each girl praying that the long hours of practice would pay off.

Cara Walker went through her three cheers with perfection, having been exhaustively coached by the co-captain of the squad.

Sandra Bacon did the same, Jessica was happy to note.

One by one, the aspirants skipped out in front of the five cheerleaders and did their routines, starting with the "Go, Gladiators" cheer, then doing two cheers of their choice and finishing up with a split.

"The split's what separates the 'want-tos' from the 'can-dos,'" Helen Bradley told Jessica, and she was right, of course. Of the twenty-five girls, more than half couldn't manage the split.

But Annie Whitman wasn't one of those. Annie was a "can-do" all the way.

Out she dashed, creating an immediate electric excitement in everybody watching—with one exception, of course.

Annie carried pom-poms, which weren't required, but which gave her an edge right away. Then she did the first two cheers with such zest and perfection that Robin Wilson actually applauded.

And when she sailed across the gym in the last cheer and did two cartwheels and a back flip and *then* a split, she was quite simply a sensation.

By then everyone was applauding, except Jessica, who pretended to be busy marking the list of names.

Annie leaped up, blushing prettily at the applause, and dashed straight to the one person who was unimpressed.

"How'd I do?" Annie asked eagerly, still not realizing she was asking the wrong person.

Jessica forced a weak smile. "We'll see," she said.

Ricky Capaldo ran over to Annie at the same time and congratulated her. Annie was radiant; she knew she had done well.

After the rest of the girls had gone through their cheers and left the gym, Ricky handed out the scoring sheets to Robin, Helen, Jean West, Maria Santelli, and Jessica. Jessica was sure everything was arranged. She had not let a day go by without telling the other cheerleaders that

Cara and Sandy were right for the team and that Annie most emphatically was not.

"She's not our type." Jessica had never missed an opportunity to drum it into their heads.

The squad sat down and made up their lists, and then Ricky read off the top eight.

Cara Walker and Sandra Bacon were on it, as Jessica had planned.

But heading the list was the name that almost made her choke.

Annie Whitman!

"There must be a mistake," Jessica cried.

Ricky checked the vote tallies. "No, no mistake," he said.

Jessica felt her toes getting red, and then her legs and her body and finally her head. She thought she would explode! How could they be so blind to the kind of person Annie was? Jessica wondered angrily. In spite of everything, she had not yet gotten across the message. But, fortunately, it wasn't too late.

Ricky Capaldo took a lot of teasing as manager of the cheerleaders. "Seven girls at a time, Capaldo," the guys said.

"Only five at the moment," said Ricky, blushing like crazy.

"Poor kid," they would say. "Only five!"

But the truth was, Ricky was very shy and hardly spoke to any of the girls in school except the cheerleaders. And that was more or less business. He kept pretty much to himself, except when he was racing wildly around the basketball court or football field helping the cheerleaders during games and practices. And even though he was quite close to the cheerleaders, Ricky would never have dreamed of asking one of them out. It was enough that he could be around them and be their friend.

But something was happening to Ricky lately. He was beginning to feel differently about one of the cheerleaders. Or at least, a girl who he felt sure would be a cheerleader very soon.

And that's why he was so happy the next day when he slipped a note to Annie Whitman in Spanish class. Annie shot a quick, excited look at Ricky and slipped the note into her Spanish book.

When class finally ended, a million years later, Annie darted outside, tore the book open, and devoured the note. "Congratulations on being one of the eight finalists," it read.

The corridor was full of Sweet Valley students on their way from one class to another. They were all treated to an explosive shriek of joy from Annie. They saw her grab Ricky Capaldo and hug him long and hard while dancing him around the hall.

"Heyyyyyyy!" Ricky laughed, red as a beet.

"Oh, Rickeeeee!" Annie yelled.

And for days after that, every time Ricky Capaldo walked into a classroom or the lunchroom, he was greeted by his fellow students with a loud chorus:

"Oh, Rickeeeee!"

Ricky could only shake his head and blush and laugh. He felt happier than he could ever remember.

Annie Whitman also felt happier than she could ever remember. She could feel her life changing day by day. Something brand new was happening to her. For one thing, her grades were climbing, and she now knew she could do as well as anybody else. For that, she had Elizabeth to thank.

But there was more to it than that. When she was doing cheers, and doing them well, she felt confident. She felt liked. Admired.

Elizabeth joined her sitting on the steps after school the day Annie had learned she had made the eight finalists.

"It's funny," Annie said, "but I'm beginning to feel a lot differently about myself. I used to think I wasn't much, Liz."

"That's silly," Elizabeth said solicitously.

"Maybe. But now I'm beginning to think I'm not so bad after all. When they applauded me, I felt that I was even respected."

"Well, you are," said Elizabeth.

"I think I'm going to cut down on my dating," Annie said. "I used to need a lot of attention. You know, to make up for that empty feeling inside. But boys aren't always the answer. I've made a lot of mistakes with boys, I guess."

Elizabeth let that one go by silently.

"How do you do it, Liz?" Annie asked, a note of sadness and envy creeping into her voice.

"How do I do what, Annie?" Elizabeth was startled by her friend's quick change in mood.

"How do you have a—a friendship—a relationship like you have with Todd Wilkins? I mean you two always seem to be having so much fun. I've never had that kind of thing with a guy."

Elizabeth remembered how it had been when she first knew Todd. She remembered how miserable she'd felt when she thought Todd was interested in Jessica and how wonderful she'd felt when she knew that Todd loved her, not her sister.

"I think it takes time to develop a good relationship, Annie. Time and trust and respect."

"I don't think any boy I've known has respected me," Annie said quietly. "And I don't think I've ever respected any of them. But that's all over now. I'm a different person now. I'm *almost* a Sweet Valley High cheerleader!"

Annie's words were still ringing in Elizabeth's ears an hour later, when she met Enid at the Dairi Burger. She was trying hard not to think about the whole cheerleading mess, but she sensed trouble and couldn't push the feeling aside.

Enid stirred her chocolate milkshake with the end of her straw and studied Elizabeth with a worried expression. "Liz, you look frazzled. Is something wrong?"

Elizabeth shook her head and gave her friend a weak smile. "No, I'm OK, Enid. Just a little tired. I've been kind of busy. . . ." Her sentence trailed off. She needed to talk about Jessica and Annie, but she didn't want to burden Enid with a problem no one could solve.

The two girls were sitting in a back booth, away from the usual crowd of kids from Sweet Valley High. Enid shifted uncomfortably in her seat and said softly, "Liz, I feel like we haven't had a chance to talk much recently." A note of hurt crept into her voice. "Don't you have time for me anymore?"

"Oh, Enid," Elizabeth said. "You're my best friend in the whole world. I always have time for you. Please, please believe me." She reached across the table to touch Enid's hand. "I guess I've been preoccupied lately. I didn't mean to ignore you. You know you're one of the most special people in my life."

Enid smiled. "Thanks, Liz. I feel the same way about you. But I'm still worried. What's bothering you? Is it something to do with Todd?"

"Todd? No, Todd and I are fine." Her face lit up as she pictured his irresistible smile. If only Annie had someone who cared about her that way, she wouldn't need Jessica and the cheerleaders quite so much. Elizabeth's expression darkened again as she thought about the problem.

She debated with herself. Should she tell Enid about Annie and Jessica? She felt it would somehow be disloyal to her sister, and she knew there wasn't much that Enid could do. But she could trust Enid to understand. And she had to talk to someone, or she was going to burst.

Pushing her half-eaten burger aside, Elizabeth leaned across the little table. "Enid, you know I've been helping Annie Whitman with math."

"You've mentioned it a few times."

"She's really a nice kid in a lot of ways."

"If you think so, I'm sure it's true."

"But have you heard any stories about her, Enid? Stories about her and boys, I mean?" Elizabeth didn't really want to hear the answer to her question, but she had to ask.

"Stories—at our school?" Enid rolled her eyes in mock surprise. "I hear they're going to change the name to Rumor Valley High any day now."

Elizabeth laughed for the first time that day. She could always count on Enid to cheer her up. But then, becoming serious again, she sighed and said, "Then you *have* heard talk about Annie?"

Enid hesitated, then said, "Yeah, I've heard all the dirt about her. But you know the way the rumor mill works, Liz. If at first nobody believes a rumor, exaggerate it. Then everybody will believe it." There was a bitter note in Enid's voice, and Elizabeth knew she was speaking from experience. A long time ago, Enid had gotten involved with a bad bunch of kids, and the gossip had nearly destroyed her.

"Hey, I'm sorry, Enid," Elizabeth said, reaching again to touch her friend's hand.

"No problem, Liz," Enid reassured her. "That part of my life is over. The girl who had all those problems doesn't exist anymore. I feel terrific. And George thinks I'm kind of OK, too," she added lightly. Her green eyes sparkled when she mentioned her boyfriend's name.

"He sure does," Elizabeth confirmed with a laugh. "And you *are* terrific."

"Yeah, I am. And so are you. But now that we've agreed that we're both absolutely out of this world," she said, growing serious again, "why are you so tense?"

Elizabeth looked down at the remains of her burger, deciding how much to tell Enid.

"Annie wants something very badly, and somehow I've gotten myself involved in helping," she confessed. "Am I being stupid?"

"That's hard to say, since I don't know what you're helping her with, besides math."

"Nothing really," Elizabeth began. "But the grades are important to Annie, because it means she can try out for the cheerleading squad. She wants that more than anything in the universe, Enid. She's trying to change her life, and she thinks being a cheerleader is the key."

"That's good, Liz. Everyone has the right to change. And if Annie keeps her grades up, I don't see where the problem is. I saw her at those tryouts you dragged me to. She's a natural."

Elizabeth hesitated before saying, "Her grades are fine—now—and she *is* a natural for the squad, but I'm afraid some people might hold her reputation against her."

"*Some* people?" Enid knew that if Elizabeth was having troubles, "some people" was undoubtedly spelled J-E-S-S-I-C-A. But she held her tongue. Elizabeth was fiercely loyal when it came to her twin, and Enid didn't want to get into an argument over the person she now realized was at the bottom of her friend's dilemma.

"What are you thinking, Enid?"

"I'm thinking that Annie is the only one who can change her own life. She has to want it, and she has to work at it."

"You're right, I know," Elizabeth said, wishing she didn't feel so helpless.

"But a good friend can help," Enid added. "Sometimes I don't know what I would do without your support, Liz. Annie's lucky. She's got you on her side."

Maybe it wasn't hopeless after all, Elizabeth thought.

Six

Annie Whitman would have felt a lot less confident and happy if she could have known what was going on in Jessica Wakefield's mind.

Somehow, despite Jessica's best efforts, Easy Annie had made it to the final tryout. She'd even managed to get her grades up, with the help of that sly traitor, Elizabeth Benedict Arnold Wakefield, Jessica thought.

But nothing more would be left to chance. Annie's flashy first appearance, her show-off exhibition the second time, her grades, her good looks, her dancing ability—none of them meant a thing unless she could get three of the five cheerleaders to vote for her.

Jessica had steered Helen Bradley away from school, avoiding the Dairi Burger, to Casey's Place over at the mall for this high-level strategy session.

Sipping a diet soda paid for by Jessica, Helen

was alert to what was obviously a highly important meeting.

"Helen," Jessica said sternly, "the image and the very integrity of the cheerleading squad are in terrible danger."

"What happened?" Helen asked, her eyes widening.

"Annie Whitman. That's what happened."

"Oh," Helen said thoughtfully.

"You know what kind of girl she is. Your own brother won't have anything to do with her anymore."

Helen looked into her soda and said nothing.

"You've seen her strutting around, haven't you?" Jessica demanded. "Out with Bruce Patman one night, with that Rick Andover the next. It's one guy after another."

"Yes," said Helen.

"If she gets on the cheering squad, everybody will think we're just like her!"

"Oh, no!" Helen said.

"They will! Birds of a feather flock together. I just wanted to find out how you feel about it. Who would you like to see on the team?"

"Well . . ." Helen thought. "Let's see."

"Cara Walker has been terrific, don't you think?"

"Oh, yes," Helen said. "It would be great to have her back on the team."

"Well, then, can I count on your vote for Cara?" Jessica asked.

"Oh, sure." Helen was relieved to find out that was all. Except that it wasn't.

"OK," Jessica went on. "Now for the second girl. Who would you like for the second one?"

"Well . . ."

"Isn't Sandra Bacon a good choice?"

Yes, Helen agreed, Sandra was great. "Only . . ."

Jessica frowned. "Only what?"

"Well, Jess, I like Sandy a lot. But do you think she can beat out Annie?"

Jessica let out an exasperated breath. "Helen, of course she can! If three of us vote for her."

Helen sipped her soda and pondered that. "You mean even if Annie is better, we can vote in Sandra?"

Jessica sat back and let that idea float across the booth and through Helen's head.

"Whoever gets three votes is in," Jessica said.

"Yes, that's true," Helen mused. "I wonder who the others will vote for?"

Jessica glanced at Helen and decided to set her grand plan in motion. "Helen, the fact is that it's entirely up to one person. One person can uphold the squad or let it all go down the drain."

"Really? Who?" Helen asked.

"You. Helen Bradley, that's who. You have everything in your hands. I hope you won't let down your squad or your school."

Helen felt herself tingling with importance and confusion. She'd never expected this!

"But I don't understand, Jess," she said, bewildered.

"It's very simple, Helen," Jessica explained. "It takes three votes to be selected, right?"

70

"Right," said Helen.

"OK. I'm going to vote for Sandy Bacon. That's one vote. Now, tell me who is Sandra Bacon's very best friend in the entire school who also happens to be on the cheerleading squad?"

"Oh, sure—Jeanie West."

"Right," said Jessica. "So Sandra Bacon has my vote and Jeanie West's vote for certain. She needs only one more."

"Yeah," said Helen, realizing the meaning of it.

"Your vote will decide, Helen."

Helen shoved her glass away and looked out over the mall. "Oh, wow," she said. "You're right."

It was all very simple, Jessica told herself with satisfaction. No one could be sure of what Robin Wilson would do. And Maria Santelli simply kept raving about Annie Whitman so much that it looked as if her vote was lost.

But now it didn't matter.

"Will you promise to vote for Cara and Sandra?" Jessica pressed her.

"Well . . . OK," Helen said.

"I'll tell Jeanie that we'll both vote for Sandra and Cara, if she will, too."

"Then it's all fixed," Helen said.

Jessica smiled sweetly. "Yes, and you decided the whole thing."

Unaware that Jessica was maneuvering the final vote so that she could never become a cheerleader, Annie Whitman continued to grow more confident, and a new sort of person was blossoming within her. For the first time, she noticed that quiet Ricky Capaldo shot looks at her in Spanish class and in the cafeteria. When she caught him, he always blushed violently and looked away.

After Spanish she often walked alongside Ricky and tried to talk casually, but he seemed uncomfortable and tongue-tied. Once, he started to relax, and the natural, friendly side of him was just coming out when somebody spotted them, and the next thing Annie knew a loud chorus of "Oh, Rickeeeee!" had him more flushed than ever.

"How do you get a shy boy to talk to you?" Annie asked Elizabeth one day as school was letting out.

Elizabeth laughed. "I didn't think you had any trouble getting anybody to talk."

"Oh, I don't. Not most of them, anyway. Bruce Patman calls me up all the time, but I've decided I don't like him. I've been waiting for a different type of boy to ask me out. I'm waiting for one particular *different* boy."

"Watch what you say, Annie," Elizabeth teased as the two girls strolled across the Sweet Valley campus in the warm afternoon sunshine. "Remember you're in the presence of the writer of the 'Eyes and Ears' column."

"Oh, Liz," Annie pleaded, "you wouldn't use this in your column. You couldn't!"

"Not if you don't want me to use it, Annie,"

Elizabeth said with concern. "Hey, we're friends, right?"

"*You* want to be *my* friend?" Annie asked. "Somebody like you would be a friend to somebody like me?" The look of surprise and delight on Annie's face touched Elizabeth.

"Of course we're friends, Annie. But I thought we were talking about boys. Who is this *different* guy you're interested in?"

"Ricky."

"Ricky Capaldo? Don't I remember something about him being just a pal?"

Annie blushed. "I know, but I'm seeing him in a new way. He's so nice, Liz. He's so sweet and friendly, and I don't know—do you know what I mean?"

"Of course I know what you mean," Elizabeth assured her.

"But he doesn't ask me out. And neither do some of the other nice guys. I wonder why not."

This time there was no doubt left in Elizabeth's mind. Annie was totally unaware of what people thought of her. The next minute Elizabeth discovered she was on the spot.

"Have you ever heard anybody talk about me?" said Annie shyly. She and Elizabeth stopped in the shade of an oak tree.

"Well . . ." Elizabeth hesitated. "Everybody gets talked about." She placed her books on the grass as she sat down near the tree, Annie settling beside her.

"Sure. They talk about you as a writer and

73

the nicest girl in Sweet Valley. But what do they say about me?"

"Listen, what difference does it make? You know that the only thing that matters is how you feel about yourself."

"That's true." Annie brightened. "And people can change, can't they? And when you change and make yourself into a different person, people accept that, don't they?"

"Absolutely," Elizabeth said firmly. "If they're decent people, they do."

"Thanks," Annie said. "I always feel so much better after talking to you. Just think, when I finally get on the cheerleading team, there'll be a brand-new me at Sweet Valley High."

And before Elizabeth knew what was happening, Annie leaned over and hugged her. Then she jumped up and hurried off across the wide campus lawn.

Later, when Elizabeth reached the Wakefields' split-level house, she was humming to herself and feeling good all over at Annie's success. It wasn't easy for a person to turn her life around the way Annie was doing.

Coming in through the living room, Elizabeth heard laughter from the patio out back near the swimming pool. She strolled out to find Jessica serving Cokes to Jeanie West and Helen Bradley.

"Well, well," said Elizabeth, "the ears of every boy in town must be burning. And half the girls."

"Oh, go jump in the pool." Jessica laughed contentedly.

"So, what's happening?" Elizabeth asked. "Anything I can print?"

"You could, but you won't." Jessica grinned mysteriously.

"Oh?"

"Because you *never* print anything in advance, even though it's an absolutely, positively sure thing," said Jessica. "Am I right?" she asked the other two, and they all laughed like conspirators in on a big secret.

Elizabeth didn't like what she saw. "I would just take a wild guess that this little gathering has something to do with who the new cheerleaders are going to be," she said.

The three laughed again, but made no comment. At that moment Elizabeth knew with certainty that the two new cheerleaders would be Cara Walker and Sandra Bacon.

Elizabeth felt her breath go out like a beach ball deflating. What could she say? Cara and Sandy were certainly good choices, and it really wasn't any of Elizabeth's business; she wasn't even on the squad. Still, she felt a terrible sense of dread at the thought of how Annie would take it.

"Well?" Jessica challenged her twin. "Would you like to make a bet on this one, Liz?"

Elizabeth shook her head, and walked unhappily back into the house. This was another bet she knew she couldn't win.

* * *

Later that afternoon, Elizabeth and Todd were sitting on the sofa in the family room of the Wilkins home, watching an old movie on TV. The smell of homemade cake wafted in from the kitchen, where Mrs. Wilkins was preparing dinner.

Elizabeth snuggled closer to Todd, trying hard to concentrate on the movie. But her thoughts kept turning to Annie and Jessica. Without being fully aware of it, she heaved a loud sigh.

"OK, Wakefield. Out with it." Todd sat straight up on the sofa and looked searchingly into Elizabeth's blue-green eyes.

"Out with what?" Elizabeth asked.

"What's on your mind? You're hardly paying any attention to the movie. Are you bored? You want to see what else is on?"

"No, this is—fine," Elizabeth said falteringly.

"But *you're* not fine. Come on, Liz, it's me, Todd. I thought you could tell me anything."

"Oh, Todd. It's nothing. I guess my thoughts were someplace else."

He unfolded his long frame, stood, and walked over to flip off the set.

"That's been happening a lot lately. Are your thoughts some*place* else, or on some*one* else?"

Someone else? Todd couldn't think that! She hadn't been interested in another guy since the day she met Todd.

She looked at Todd's back. He wouldn't face her. Elizabeth rose slowly from the sofa, walked over to Todd, and put her hand on his arm. "Todd, please look at me!"

It seemed like forever, but Todd finally turned toward Elizabeth. His mouth was set and grim.

"How could you think that there was some-one else? You know how I feel about you, Todd." She put up a hand to touch his cheek.

"I know how *I* feel about *you*, Liz," he said, not moving to touch her. "I know I love you. I thought you loved me."

"Oh, Todd." She sighed, wrapping her arms around his waist and pulling him close to her. "I love you. You have to believe that."

Elizabeth felt Todd as he put his strong arms around her, hugging her tightly. "When we hold each other like this, I believe you. But you had me scared."

"Scared? You? The star basketball player of Sweet Valley High is scared by little old me?" she teased. "I'd better run right down to the *Oracle* office and have them stop the presses."

Todd's response was a tender kiss. "If the opposing team had five beautiful blonds ex-actly like you, I'd be helpless," he confessed when they finished their embrace. "But that'd be impossible, because there *is* no one exactly like you, Liz."

Todd moved back to the sofa, Elizabeth set-tling next to him. He placed a large hand on her knee and then said sternly, "OK, Elizabeth Wakefield, talk."

"Talk?"

"You're not in love with someone else."

"Never!"

"But something is driving you up the wall, right?"

Elizabeth wished he weren't so quick to sense when she was upset.

"Not really, Todd. It's just that I've been busy with—with things." That didn't sound believable even to her. She silently cursed herself for getting so involved with the cheering tryouts that she had neglected the people she cared about most—first Enid, now Todd.

"Things," Todd repeated. "These things don't by some strange chance have to do with your perfect, saintly sister, do they?" he asked bitingly.

Elizabeth bolted up from the sofa, hands on her hips.

"There you go again, Todd Wilkins," she accused. "You really have it in for Jess!" She didn't want Todd to know about Jessica's vendetta against Annie. And she didn't want him to know how committed she was to Annie's cause. Todd would only chide her for allowing Jessica to get her into another mess.

"I'm right! Jess *is* up to something, and you're going to stick your neck out for her. Don't you ever get tired of rescuing your sister?"

"You are an insensitive—"

"Jock," he finished.

They glared at each other angrily.

"Hello?" It was Mrs. Wilkins. She stepped into the family room.

"Mom, we're having a discussion," Todd said without looking at his mother.

Mrs. Wilkins gave a knowing look at the two tense figures.

"Discussions are fine," she said wryly. "But in the interest of the cake in the oven, keep the *discussion* down to a low roar, OK?"

Some of the tension went out of the room with her words.

"Your mom is nice," Elizabeth said as Mrs. Wilkins went back into the kitchen.

"It runs in the family," Todd said.

"I know." Elizabeth smiled at him, wishing she could pour out the whole complicated situation to Todd. She had to help Annie, yet she also had to protect Jessica. Todd would understand about Annie, she was sure, but protecting Jessica was not one of the things that was high on his list. Telling him would simply start another argument.

"You're not going to tell me what's bothering you, are you?"

"I wish I could, Todd. I just can't, not right now." Pleading for understanding, she tilted her face up toward his.

"OK, Liz. You know that when you look at me like that, I'll agree to anything. Just remember, I'm on your side. I'll help whenever you need me." He lowered his head and kissed her. Suddenly Jessica and Annie seemed far away.

Seven

Something strange was happening to Ricky
Capaldo. When he studied the Revolutionary
War and its causes, music drifted into his mind.
And not some fife-and-drum march leading
Washington's troops toward Valley Forge, either.
No, Ricky's attempts at studying were being
sidetracked by love songs.

Plain-looking, shy, quiet Ricky was falling in
love with Annie Whitman, and he was terrified.
A large part of the terror was that Annie seemed
to be interested in him, too, even though Ricky
found it almost totally impossible to believe.

Annie Whitman was beautiful. Annie was a
great dancer. Annie had a million boyfriends.
How could he, a little nobody who was nothing
to look at and practically tongue-tied with girls,
ever bring himself to speak to Annie about
anything, well, romantic? Totally idiotic!

Ricky Capaldo summoned every bit of his

resolve and banished all thoughts of Annie from his mind.

"The three major causes of the Revolutionary War," he noted in his book, "were a denial of basic rights, the Stamp Act, and Annie Whitman."

Ricky threw down his ball-point pen.

Not only was it impossible for him to believe that a dazzling beauty like Annie would be interested in him, but there was also the problem of all those stories about her. Were they true? he wondered agonizingly.

Forget it, he told himself sternly and returned to the Revolutionary War. Minutemen were marching across Concord Green playing "I Can't Smile Without You."

There was a pretty good turnout of students for the cheerleading finals. Most of the girls who had already been cut were there to see who among the final eight would get the two vacant spots on the squad.

Once again, Ricky Capaldo was all over the gym arranging things, handing out score sheets to the five cheerleaders, and telling the finalists when they were to go on. Everybody knew it was pretty much down to three girls—Cara Walker, Sandra Bacon, and Annie Whitman. The finalists went on alphabetically, so Sandra was the first one and Annie was the last.

Needless to say, all the finalists had worked very hard on their routines, and countless practice sessions were behind them. With eight girls trying for two places, it was down to hairsplitting time. The same unspoken words were in each girl's mind: "Please don't let me make a mistake!"

For the finals, the girls had been given real cheerleader costumes—short red skirts and white sweaters with SV in big red letters on them.

Jessica watched confidently as Sandra came trotting out, looking terrific in her costume. Nothing could go wrong now, she thought, as Sandra whipped through her well-practiced routines flawlessly until she got to the final cartwheel-split finish.

And then, before Jessica's horrified eyes, Sandra did a replay of her performance at Lila Fowler's pool party.

Sanda hit the polished gym floor with her front heel, then bounced off her back foot, skidded to a halt like a jet during an emergency landing, and ended up in a heap.

"Oofffff!" went Sandra.

"Oh, no," muttered Jessica.

Red-faced, Sandra slunk past Jessica. She knew she'd blown her chances for good.

The next five girls performed their cheers without making any major mistakes, but without the style and energy that Jessica and the other cheerleaders were looking for. Then Cara Walker did her routine, making the most of her chance with a peppy performance capped with a flourish at the end. Jessica sighed with relief.

Finally came Annie Whitman. Jessica became

glummer and glummer as Annie got better and better with each move.

"Look at her," Maria Santelli cried in wonder. "I think she has wings!"

"Great," Robin Wilson agreed.

Jessica looked at Helen and Jean and smiled a knowing smile.

Once more Annie left the gym with applause ringing in her ears, a smile on her face, and tears of joy in her eyes.

"Well," Robin said after it was over, "I don't think there's much doubt. Cara and Annie are the best ones."

"Oh, yes," agreed Maria.

"Wait a minute," Jessica said. "I agree with you about Cara Walker. She's terrific, and a really great girl. In fact, I'm ready to vote on her right now."

"OK by me," Robin said. "All in favor of Cara Walker?"

All five cheerleaders raised their hands. Ricky jotted down Cara's name.

"Now, as to Annie," Jessica said, "I think we ought to remember she's only a sophomore. Sandy's a junior."

"Sandy is also a klutz," Robin said.

"Anybody can fall doing a split," Jessica retorted. "Isn't that right, Jeanie?"

"Sure," Jean West agreed. "I want Sandra!"

"Sandy's your best friend, Jeanie," Maria said. "But be honest. Isn't Annie better?"

"I'm voting for Sandra," Jean insisted.

"Now, listen, everyone," said Jessica, "there's more at stake here than just looking good."

The other cheerleaders frowned. The subject of Annie's reputation had never been openly discussed.

"We're not just cheerleaders. We're examples," Jessica went on.

"Those stories may just be rumors," Robin countered, defending Annie. "I'm voting for Annie, and that's final." Robin knew from a past experience, what it was like to have Jessica as an enemy. She hoped she could spare Annie the pain Jessica could cause.

"Well, I'm voting against Annie—I mean, I'm voting for Sandy Bacon," Jessica said. "And that's just as final."

"I'm for Sandy, too," Jeanie West said. "OK. I admit it. She's my best friend."

"I'm for Annie," Maria said.

"Well, that makes it two and two so far," Jessica said.

Usually Ricky Capaldo kept quiet during the voting, but now the girls were surprised to hear him speak up for Annie.

"Listen, I know I don't get to vote. But the squad is just as important to me as it is to you," he said. "I think Annie would make a terrific cheerleader. I hope you give her a chance."

"You betcha," Maria said.

Jessica, listening with growing annoyance, was glad she had left nothing to chance this time. The girls were looking at Helen Bradley.

"Helen, you aren't going to tell me you think Sandy is better than Annie," Robin challenged.

"Well . . ." Helen hedged.

"Did you *see* Annie?" Maria Santelli jumped in. "Why, she was a ballerina!"

"I know." Helen sighed. "She's the best I've ever seen."

Jessica's voice filled the gym like a clap of thunder. "Helen Bradley!"

Helen looked away and then back at a glowering Jessica. "Well, I know, Jess, but Annie really is something. And Sandy messed up," she added plaintively. "You saw her! She won't expect to beat out Annie after that. You know she won't."

"Well," Robin Wilson said, smiling. "Then it looks like we have three votes for Annie Whitman. She's in."

"Wait a minute," Jessica declared, her face red and trembling. "We've all been tippytoeing around the most important thing here, and you know it! Why do you think I want to keep Annie off this squad? Because if we take her, everybody will think we're just like her. Everyone will think we're as bad as Easy Annie."

Jessica's words filled the gym. Annie's extraordinary talent had overshadowed all the rumors about her, but now Jessica was dragging them out into the open, demanding they be looked at and weighed and judged.

Ricky Capaldo felt an unbearable pain searing his insides as Jessica made her accusation.

He closed his eyes and tried not to listen. But Jessica wasn't through yet.

"We've voted Cara Walker onto the squad. That's fine. Now we vote for Sandra Bacon or for Annie Whitman. I just want everybody to know that if you vote for Annie, you'll have to find another cheerleader as well. Because you won't have me anymore. Jessica Wakefield will not be on a cheerleading squad with Easy Annie."

"But, Jess!" wailed a distraught Helen Bradley. "You're the heart and soul of the squad. Without you, it wouldn't be the Sweet Valley cheerleaders at all!"

"Make your choice," Jessica said. "It's either me or Easy Annie."

Eight

As soon as she heard the front door slam, Elizabeth tossed aside her history book and jumped up from her bed. Like a shot, she was out of the room and down the stairs.

"Jess!"

Jessica was in the kitchen pouring herself a glass of milk when her sister reached her.

"What happened?" Elizabeth asked eagerly.

Jessica smiled innocently. "What happened where?"

"Come on, Jess, out with it."

"Well," Jessica said, talking a gulp of milk, "we voted."

"And?"

"And I dropped off the list of the new cheerleaders in the box at the *Oracle* office, as I promised."

"Jessica Wakefield!" Elizabeth wailed. "You know I won't see your note until tomorrow morning. Now tell me who got picked?"

Jessica cocked her head as though in surprise. "But, Elizabeth, you don't want to know in advance, do you?"

"It isn't in advance anymore. Who was chosen?"

Jessica giggled. "That's for me to know and you to find out."

"Oh, are you asking for it!" Elizabeth fumed.

Jessica smiled maddeningly. "The best ones were selected."

"Really?" Elizabeth asked hopefully. Did that mean that Jessica had come to her senses and voted for Annie? "Well, who did you vote for?"

"It took a lot of thought," Jessica said with studied seriousness. "Finally, I voted for Pat Benetar!"

"Ahhhhhhhhhh!" Elizabeth exploded and was advancing around the counter toward her tormentor when they heard a car door slam.

"There's Mom and Dad," Elizabeth said. "Did you see their note? They want to talk to us as soon as possible."

"What's doing?"

Elizabeth shrugged. "Got me."

Ned and Alice Wakefield were talking excitedly as they entered the house. When they reached the kitchen area, they both stopped and looked at the twins and then at each other.

"OK, who tells them?" Ned Wakefield asked.

"You can."

"Girls, we've got some news."

"You're going to love it," said their mother, jumping in. "Wait till you hear."

"What?" Jessica asked eagerly.

"What's going on?" Elizabeth urged.

"Actually, it's going to be kind of a difficult choice," Alice Wakefield said. "Ned, you tell them."

"I'm trying to," said their father. "OK—"

"We're going to have a house guest," Mrs. Wakefield interrupted.

"I thought you wanted me to tell them," Ned Wakefield reminded his wife.

"You take too long," Alice Wakefield said.

"A house guest?" Jessica cried. "Anybody terrific like—a rock star?"

"You wish," their father drawled.

Their mother laughed. "Now, Jess, be serious. You remember your father talking about Tom Devlin, his roommate at college who became a diplomat?"

"An ambassador is coming to stay?" said Elizabeth.

"Not Tom, honey, his daughter Suzanne."

"She's just your age," their father said. "It'll be like having another sister in the house."

"Hey, wow," Jessica exclaimed. "Suzanne Devlin! Don't they live in New York?"

"Yes," said Alice Wakefield.

"And Paris?" Elizabeth added.

"And in London, too," said Ned Wakefield.

"Boy, she's been all over," Elizabeth said.

"Wow, a really sophisticated New Yorker who's lived in Paris and London?" Even Jessica was impressed.

"She's beautiful, too," Ned Wakefield said.

Elizabeth laughed. "She would be."

"Anyway," their father said, with a glance at his wife, "if I'm allowed to get a word in here . . . Suzanne will be here for two weeks."

"That'll be fun," Elizabeth said. "We can find out all about New York!"

The twins' parents were looking at each other slyly and smiling again. Mrs. Wakefield whispered to Mr. Wakefield. He whispered back.

"What's going on?" said Jessica.

"There's more?" Elizabeth wanted to know.

"There's more," said their mother. "A lot more. But—"

"Uh-oh," Jessica moaned. "There had to be a 'but'!"

"It's good," said their mother, laughing. "But part of it's better than the other part."

"Boy, you two ought to be diplomats yourselves," Elizabeth said.

"While Suzanne Devlin is here with us, one of you will go to New York for the same two weeks," said Mrs. Wakefield. "There, it's out."

Jessica and Elizabeth looked at each other in astonishment.

"One of us?" Elizabeth asked.

"But which one?" Jessica asked.

"We're not going to decide that right now," Alice Wakefield said. "But either way, it should be fun. One of you will get to show Suzanne Devlin around Sweet Valley, and the other will see New York."

"Liz is already a lot more sophisticated than I

am," Jessica said. "So I think I need the New York trip the most."

"Jess," Elizabeth countered, "you are about as unsophisticated as a mink coat."

Alice Wakefield laughed. "We're not deciding now, so you can both compose yourselves."

"It's not fair!" Jessica wailed. "I won't be able to sleep for days! I can't stand secrets!"

"You can't stand secrets," Elizabeth remarked after their parents had retired to the study and she and Jessica were on their way back upstairs. "But you won't tell me who you picked for the cheerleader squad."

"Later, Liz, later. I have just had the most sensational idea!"

"Oh, no," Elizabeth groaned. "Not another one of your sensational ideas. It could mean disaster."

"Not this one," Jessica insisted as she sat down on her sister's bed. "You are going to flip over this one, I promise."

"OK, Jess, out with it."

"Suzanne and Steven!" Jessica announced with the air of someone who has just discovered the secrets of the universe.

Elizabeth stared at her. "Look at me closely, Jess. I am not flipping. And do you know *why* I am not flipping? It is because you, sister dear, are not making any sense."

Jessica shot Elizabeth a look of disgust. "I really hate it when you talk to me like that, you know? If you would just take a minute to think about my idea, you would see how good it is.

Suzanne Devlin is beautiful, talented, intelligent, and sophisticated," Jessica pointed out.

"So?"

"So? You are deliberately being dense, Liz. Our visitor is the perfect girl to lure our brother away from Tricia Martin!"

"Do you have a death wish, Jess?" Elizabeth asked. "Steven would take you apart if you butted into his relationship with Tricia."

"Not if you helped me," Jessica suggested, reluctant to give up her plan.

"No, Jess, no way. Forget it," Elizabeth said, shaking her head. "Tricia is sweet and lovely and a terrific girl for Steve. I absolutely refuse to take your side against her. Case closed. And now let's get back to the real subject."

"What subject is that?" Jessica asked innocently.

"About how you can't stand secrets but won't tell me who the second new cheerleader is."

"Oh, that's different." Jessica pouted. "*I* already *know* that secret."

"Jessica, you are being impossible!"

"OK." Jessica grinned. "I'll tell you half. We picked Cara Walker."

Jessica's self-satisfied little smile was suddenly buried under a pillow expertly thrown by her sister.

"OK, Liz, you asked for it."

Jessica grabbed a pillow and charged. Elizabeth retaliated. Wham! Crash! The twins blasted each other, laughing wildly the whole time, tumbling over Elizabeth's bed.

Downstairs, Alice Wakefield sighed. "Do you suppose they're still fighting about who the more sophisticated one is?"

To Elizabeth's astonishment, Jessica never did reveal the outcome of the cheering tryouts. It was practically the only time she could remember Jessica keeping any kind of a secret more than five minutes. When she went to sleep, Elizabeth was still wondering who the other new cheerleader was.

The secret of who had been chosen for the Sweet Valley High cheering squad caused even more suspense for another person at Sweet Valley High that night.

Annie Whitman tossed and turned and woke up again and again. She slept fitfully, dreaming of one cheer after another and waiting impatiently for the night to end.

Finally, another day began at Sweet Valley High. Annie knew she would get the note telling her if she was in or out during her fourth-period Spanish class, because that was the class she had with Ricky Capaldo. The first three periods seemed to last forever.

When he arrived at Spanish class, Ricky lingered outside until it was almost time for the bell. Then he slipped in and handed Annie her note at the last second.

Annie grabbed the little white envelope with a shaky hand and slid it into her book. Several times during the class period, she started to open it and read the message, but each time she stopped and told herself to wait until class was over.

After all, it wouldn't do to leap up and do a cartwheel right down the aisle, she decided, laughing to herself.

She just *had* to have made the squad. Every one of her appearances had been a triumph, and Sandra Bacon had clearly put herself out of contention when she tripped.

I'm almost a cheerleader! A real Sweet Valley High cheerleader! Annie told herself over and over.

Annie peeked shyly across at Ricky Capaldo, but for once he was not looking at her. Ricky was staring straight down at his book.

Only after what seemed like endless hours did the bell ring to end the class. Annie sat rigidly at her seat until the other kids had gone out, and then she dashed out into the corridor, put her books down on the floor, and ripped open the little note.

It read:

"We are sorry to inform you that you have not been selected for the Sweet Valley High cheering squad this year. Thanks for trying, and good luck next time!"

Nine

Annie stood against the wall in the corridor, in a state of shock. The note slipped from her fingers and fluttered to the floor.

"They didn't pick me?" she was finally able to ask herself in a stupor. Who else had been better? Who could possibly have been chosen over her?

Annie glanced down at the message on the floor. She leaned down to pick it up and turned it over to look at the words again.

The note hadn't changed.

Annie crumpled the paper into a tight little ball in her fist. She swayed and thought she might faint. She felt nauseated. Seconds passed. Minutes. Hours. Years.

They don't want me? she wondered to herself. *But I was good! I was the best one there!*

In her mind's eye, Annie saw herself sailing through her cheers, felt the audience's eyes on her, heard the applause. They were clapping for her. Because she was good. The applause rang in her ears. She heard something else, too—a voice, far away, in the back of her daydream.

Annie felt paralyzed, unable to move. She stood there, held by the applause, the object of the audience's attention. The voice spoke again, this time from closer.

"Are you all right?"

Annie spun around. She saw Ricky Capaldo standing beside her, looking into her face with concern.

"All right?" she parroted. She felt as if she'd never be all right again.

"I'm really sorry, Annie."

Annie saw the pity in Ricky's face, and she couldn't bear it another second. With a cry, she turned on her heel and rushed down the corridor, not bothering to pick up her books from the floor.

"Annie!" Ricky called after her.

She rushed to the staircase, down the stairs, and into the front hall. She dashed down the wide steps and across the green expanse of lawn.

"Wait!" she heard a voice calling.

But Annie did not stop running. All the way across the wide campus she raced, hardly able to see. She ran across the football field. On and on she ran, up an aisle among the vast expanse of empty bleachers.

"Annie!" The voice still followed her.

Annie ran upward until she reached the wall

at the very top of the back of the stadium, and there she could go no further. She slumped against the wall and slid to the floor of the top level, exhausted.

That's where Ricky Capaldo found her.

"Hey, who do you think you are, a marathon runner?" he said brightly.

Annie huddled against the wall, silent, breathing in quick little gasps.

Ricky knelt down beside her. "Hey, Annie," he said softly. "Come on."

"Leave me alone."

"Aw, Annie, how can I leave you alone? Way up here in the stadium all by yourself? Let's go to the Dairi Burger for lunch, huh? Come on. I'll buy you a shake. What kind do you like?"

No answer.

"Chocolate? Strawberry?"

"I worked so hard for it. How could I not get it?" Annie asked softly. "I can't believe it."

Ricky sat on the concrete beside her, trying desperately and unsuccessfully to think of some way to cheer her up.

"It isn't possible not to get something you want as much as I want this," Annie said, her voice faltering, tears streaming down her cheeks. "It . . . isn't . . . poss—possible!"

Annie put her face in her hands and cried with abandon, her body wracked with sobs. Ricky had never felt so useless. He put his arm around her and pulled her close.

Annie's head was on his chest. She leaned against him and sobbed as though her heart would surely break.

"I know," was all Ricky could say. "I know, Annie."

"Why?" Annie finally said, sniffing and looking up at him. "Why?"

"Well, there were only vacancies for two girls," Ricky said.

"Yes, but I was the best one who tried out! Wasn't I?"

"I thought you were," Ricky admitted. "But I don't get to vote. I spoke for you, honestly I did."

Annie sat up and wiped her eyes and tried to think. "It was just such a surprise," she said. "I mean, at first, I didn't think I had a chance. But then, after the first tryout and after I found out I could get my grades up, I started to think I could do it. I really started feeling differently about a lot of things."

"You were really terrific at all the tryouts," Ricky agreed.

"So who was chosen?" Annie finally dared to ask. She drew away from Ricky, her head bent in defeat.

"Cara," said Ricky. "And Sandra," he added, his voice barely a whisper.

"Well, Cara *was* good," Annie admitted, fair to the other girl even in her misery. "And she's already been part of the team. But Sandy—Sandy fell!"

Annie's voice rose at the injustice, and she pounded the wall at the top of the bleachers with her fist. Ricky sat beside her, worrying about her.

"Ricky," she said, lifting her face toward him, "who voted against me?"

"Well, let's see," Ricky said, stalling. "Robin Wilson thought you were great! And so did Maria Santelli."

"Yes," Annie said thoughtfully. "I sort of thought they were for me. Robin even applauded!" Annie's face lit up with happiness at the memory. But then hurt and misery slid back across her lovely features.

"So that means Jeanie, Helen, and Jessica voted against me." Annie shook her head in bewilderment. She could understand Jeanie West's vote, because after all she was Sandra's best friend. And perhaps Tim Bradley had said something to his sister Helen after Annie's less than terrific date with him. But what about Jessica Wakefield?

"I really thought Jessica wanted me on the squad," Annie said. "She knew I could do all the routines." She frowned and looked closely at Ricky. "Did Jessica really vote against me?"

"She voted for Sandra, that's all." Ricky looked away, turning the color of a Mexican red pepper.

Annie rose to her feet. Slowly she began dragging herself down the long stairs from the top of the stadium toward the playing field.

"I could accept it, I guess, if I just could understand," she said, pausing after two steps. She turned to face Ricky again. "Did anybody say anything?"

Ricky looked at his feet. "Aw, what's the difference?" he answered evasively.

Annie walked down two more steps and settled down on one of the long wooden bleachers.

"Sure, somebody said something," Annie stated. "I couldn't have been totally out of the running." A tiny note of pride crept its way to the surface. "Why, there must have been a regular discussion! What was the vote against me—three to two?"

Ricky got up and took her hand. "Come on. Let's go to the Dairi Burger."

"No," Annie said, pulling back. "I have to know what happened or I'll go crazy! You said Robin and Maria spoke for me."

"Sure! And so did Helen Bradley."

"What?"

"Sure! She said that when Sandra tripped, you should have been picked." Ricky was sorry as soon as the words were out of his mouth. His confession could only bring Annie more pain.

"But that would be three votes! You mean Helen changed her mind?"

"Annie, you don't want to keep going over this," Ricky protested. "It's not going to do any good. Why don't you forget it?"

"Ricky, if there were three girls for me, who talked them out of it?"

"Well . . ."

"Who?"

"Jessica."

Annie was back on her feet. She couldn't sit still. "Jessica knifed me? But why?" Her astonishment was as clear as day.

Ricky took Annie's hand as they ran down the steps, all the way to the bottom, and then out across the track and onto the field.

"Come on," he said. "Let's go get a soda and forget about it." Ricky's shyness was gone. All he could think about was easing Annie's grief.

But Annie was inconsolable. "This is where I'd be in football season," she lamented, looking around the field. "Right here! Watch this!"

And off she went, dashing along in front of the empty team bench and the huge, silent stands, swinging into one cartwheel and then another. From the cartwheels she sailed gracefully into a back flip and finished off with a split, a dazzling exhibition of grace and skill.

Ricky ran to her where she was crumpled on the grass. She was laughing as he ran up.

"That was great," he said, sinking down beside her, taking her in his arms.

Then he realized she was not laughing. She was crying.

"Ricky, if you care for me, you have to tell me what happened."

"I can't."

"You have to. If I did something wrong, I can make it right the next time. I have to know. Tell me the truth."

He did owe her the truth, Ricky decided. He'd given her half the story already, and it was probably worse for her to wonder about the rest of it than to actually know what had happened.

"Well," Ricky began hesitantly, "you see . . ."

101

"Yes? Come on, Ricky."

"Annie, you have to realize that some people just say anything about other people. Somebody told Jessica things, and I guess she believed them."

Annie's face began to color, flushing a deep red. Her voice became faint. "What do you mean?"

"Darn it, Annie, Jessica brought up the stories that some guys tell about you."

"Oh, no," Annie said, moving away from him.

"Jessica said everybody in the school knew about those stories, and that—well, that if you were a cheerleader, it would ruin the whole squad."

Annie cried out and lurched backward, tears spurting from her eyes. She shook her head frantically from side to side as though trying to shake off the words.

"No, no," she shrieked. "No! Ruin the whole squad?"

She scrambled to her feet, and once more she was running. She was blinded by her tears, but she did not slow down.

"Annie," Ricky called out, but she did not stop.

Ricky ran after her across most of the stadium field, then slowed to a stop.

Annie's figure grew smaller and smaller. And then she was gone.

Ten

Ricky called himself every name in the book. Why had he told Annie the harsh truth? *Because she wanted to know*, he told himself. But did she really?

Ricky hurried from the stadium back toward school, his face set in a worried mask, his thoughts swirling out of control. Surely, he told himself, Annie must have known what the kids were saying!

But it was clear she had *not* known. Annie's anguished face appeared before him over and over again, and the words echoed in his head: *"Ruin the whole squad?"*

Why didn't I keep my mouth shut? Ricky raged at himself.

No one at Sweet Valley High saw Annie Whitman the rest of that day. Ricky went from class to class like a sleepwalker, hardly knowing where he was. After school the cheerleaders welcomed their two new members in the gym. Ricky had to hand out outfits to Sandra Bacon and Cara Walker, along with a schedule of practices, games, and other planned appearances. He knew it wasn't fair, but he could barely stand to look at their smiling faces. It wasn't their fault, he reminded himself, but that didn't help.

Finally, out of sheer frustration, he approached Jessica. She was the only person who had the power to make things right for Annie. Or was it already too late? His feet felt like lead weights, and his heart was thumping wildly, but he had to do it. He had to talk to Jessica for Annie's sake.

"Jess, have you got a couple of minutes?"

"Sure, Ricky. What's up? A problem with the new schedules?" Jessica flashed him a smile.

Maybe she would listen to him, he thought hopefully. "It's about Annie Whitman—" he began.

Jessica was no longer smiling. "I don't want to talk about that girl," Jessica snapped. "She is not on the squad. She will never be on the squad. That's final, Ricky."

"But Jessica, you don't understand," Ricky persisted. His pleading tone called out for her sympathy. "Annie's taking this very hard."

"Well, that's just too bad," Jessica returned coldly. "We all have to learn how to handle disappointments in life, don't we?" With that, she turned and walked away, leaving Ricky feeling more dejected than ever.

He went to the mall and bought a cheerful greeting card, writing on it, "You always make my day." The next day he got to Spanish class early and put the card in an envelope on Annie's desk. It lay there untouched all through the period. Annie didn't show up.

The day after that, Annie was absent from school again. Ricky got out the entry forms the aspiring cheerleaders had filled out and found her home telephone number. But no one answered his calls.

On the third day Ricky was desperate. Coming into the cafeteria, he spotted the one person he thought might be able to help.

"Hey, Liz," he said softly, "can I talk to you?"

"Sure," Elizabeth answered. "What's up?"

"Liz," Ricky said, his voice trembling, "I'm worried about Annie."

Elizabeth nodded in sympathy. "Yeah, I can understand that."

"She hasn't been to school in three days!"

"Oh, no," said Elizabeth. "Is she ill?"

Ricky hid his face and spoke hesitantly. "Yeah, she's ill, all right. Ill from dumbness and stupidity."

The cruel words surprised Elizabeth. "I thought you liked Annie, Ricky."

"Oh, Liz, I do! Of course I do. The stupidity I'm talking about is mine!"

"Yours? What happened?"

Ricky shook his head in agony, unable at first to make the words come out. Finally he forced himself to speak. "I did about the dumbest thing possible, Liz. I told her why she was kept off the cheerleading squad."

105

Elizabeth sat quietly as Ricky continued.

"I gave it to her with both barrels. Don't ask me why! She kept questioning me about why Jessica had ruined her. Finally I told her."

Elizabeth sighed. "Poor Annie. What did she say?"

"She just ran away, Liz."

"She was never aware of the things people said about her," Elizabeth said, voicing Ricky's own suspicions.

"I figured that out," he said, his eyes watery as he looked at Elizabeth. "But too late. If I'd realized it from the beginning, I might not have said anything. I didn't think it would be such a shock."

Elizabeth put her hand over Ricky's. "You did what you thought was right, Ricky."

"Liz, you've got to talk to your sister."

"To Jess?" It was more of a statement than a question.

"You've got to. Tell her what it means to Annie."

Elizabeth looked at the heartbroken boy and was filled with pity. "OK, Ricky," she said, "I'll talk to her."

By the time Elizabeth got a chance to talk to her twin that afternoon, the story about Annie was all over the school.

"Is it true," Enid asked Elizabeth between classes, "that Jessica called Annie Whitman 'Easy Annie' to her face?"

"No, no, of course not," Elizabeth said.

"That's that I heard from Emily Mayer."

"Well, Emily's wrong."

Jessica also heard stories. In gym class Susan Stewart whispered, "Tell me about the big fight."

"What big fight?" Jessica asked, eager for gossip.

"Everybody says you and Annie Whitman had a big fight about her being a cheerleader, and you called her the tramp of the school."

Jessica allowed herself a small smile. "Is that what they're saying?" She didn't deny a thing.

"So what happened?" Susan pressed.

"What happened," Jessica said firmly, "is that she's not on the cheerleading squad."

After school Elizabeth found her sister in their pool floating on her back on a rubber raft. She put her books down and sat on the edge of the small diving board.

"Jess," she called, "I want to talk to you."

Jessica opened one eye, then closed it again. "I'm working on my tan, Liz. What is it?"

"Have you heard what they're saying about you and Annie?"

"So?"

"Is any of it possibly true? Did you call her Easy Annie to her face?"

Jessica turned over onto her stomach, being careful not to slide off into the turquoise water. She glanced at her sister. "Lizzie, do you think I'm an absolute, total beast without feelings?"

"Don't make me answer that one, Jess. Just tell me—yes or no?"

"Oh, of course I didn't. I haven't even seen her since the tryouts."

"Promise?"

"Honest. Ask Robin or any of the girls."

"Well, I'm glad that at least you didn't make the situation any worse than it already is."

Jessica paddled to the side of the pool and pulled herself out of the water onto an immense beach towel. "Whatever are you talking about?" she asked her sister as she began rubbing oil on her perfectly tanned legs.

"Jess, you know Annie was the best person to try out for the squad. You should have made her a cheerleader."

"I told you from the start there was no way Easy Annie would ever be on the squad while I was a captain," Jessica said sternly.

"But you didn't say anything to her face?"

Jessica tossed her head. "No! But the truth is the truth, Liz."

Elizabeth walked over to a little wrought-iron chair under the brilliant yellow beach umbrella and sat down near Jessica. "Jess, don't you think you could reconsider?"

"What?"

"Couldn't you let Annie on the cheering squad?"

"Elizabeth Wakefield, sometimes I think you're from another world! I just explained that—"

"Yes, but it would mean so much to her," Elizabeth interrupted.

"It means even more to us to keep the squad clean," Jessica said righteously.

"Good heavens, Jess, she's only fifteen years old! And she's trying her best to become the kind of person everyone will respect. I'm really impressed with how much she's changed during the last few weeks. The cheering squad would have a wonderful influence on her. Come on, Jess, show a little compassion."

Jessica's face grew contorted with anger. Lightning flashed from her blue-green eyes. "I am sick and tired of hearing that girl defended," she exploded. "For the last time, Annie Whitman is a disaster!"

Jessica stood up, pulled her bath towel around her, and stalked across the patio and into the house.

On Monday afternoon Alice Wakefield and the twins were sitting in the living room talking about Suzanne Devlin again and discussing which twin would go to New York and which would stay in Sweet Valley to show Suzanne around.

"We could let you draw names out of a hat," Mrs. Wakefield said.

"But I don't know whether I'd rather see New York or stay around here and be with Suzanne," Jessica moaned. "How about you, Liz?"

"Tell you what," Elizabeth said. "You do one, and I'll do the other."

"What?"

"Gotcha!"

The ring of the telephone put an end to the conversation. Elizabeth moved across the room and picked up the receiver. "Hello?"

"Elizabeth?" said an extremely distraught voice.

"Yes. Is that you, Ricky?"

"Liz, I don't know what to do!"

"What's the matter?"

It seemed a thousand years before he replied. "Liz, it's Annie!"

"Annie?"

Elizabeth automatically looked at her sister, and Jessica looked back as she heard the name.

Ricky was on the edge of losing control. "They've rushed her to the hospital," he said.

Elizabeth gasped. "Oh, no! What's happened?"

Ricky wasn't trying to hold back his grief now. Between sobs, he blurted it out:

"Liz, Annie tried to kill herself!"

Eleven

Elizabeth hung up the phone in a daze. "Oh, my God."

Jessica leaped from the sofa and dashed to her twin's side. "What is it, Liz?"

"Annie! Oh, Jess, she tried to kill herself."

"What!" Jessica's tanned face went pale with shock. "What do you mean?"

"That was Ricky Capaldo. He said Annie's been rushed to the hospital!"

Alice Wakefield was beside her daughters by this time, listening with a worried face. "Who is it? Annie? Is she a friend of yours?"

"We know her," Jessica said faintly. "She wanted to be a cheerleader."

"The poor thing!" Alice Wakefield said. "How awful."

"Jess," Elizabeth said, "we've got to go to the hospital!"

"Oh, no, not me," Jessica whispered hoarsely. "She wouldn't want me there."

"Well, *I* want you there," Elizabeth said firmly. "Mom, can we take the Fiat?"

"Yes, of course," the twins' mother answered. "But be careful."

Driving quickly through the streets of the quiet town, Elizabeth and Jessica were both lost in their own thoughts. For once, Jessica did not complain about being in the passenger seat.

"Oh, please, let it not be serious," she murmured softly. "Oh, Liz, it just can't be."

"She'll be all right, Jess. She's got to be."

Elizabeth slid the red Spider convertible into a space at the parking lot of Joshua Fowler Memorial Hospital. As the twins climbed out, they shivered at the sight of the enormous, ominous-looking building. With a glance at each other, they both remembered Elizabeth's ordeal there not too long ago.

They hurried up the long walk, through the hospital doors, and along the seemingly endless corridor to the reception area.

"Hello," said the nurse behind the desk. "What can I do for you young ladies?" It always amazed Elizabeth that nurses and doctors could seem so calm when they were surrounded with life-or-death crises.

"Annie Whitman," Elizabeth said.

The nurse looked over her files with exasperating nonchalance, then smiled at them. "I'm sorry. We have no Annie Whitman."

"They just brought her in," Elizabeth protested. "She tried to—it was an emergency."

"Oh," the nurse said. "Well, then, she might be in the Emergency Wing. Right through there."

Elizabeth led a reluctant Jessica through the large gray door at which the nurse had pointed.

The Emergency Wing was bedlam. On a stretcher just inside the door lay a man who had been hurt in an auto crash. A little boy with a stitched-up forehead sat nearby. Little knots of people sat huddled in chairs waiting for news of friends and relatives.

On one of the chairs in the crowded waiting room sat Ricky Capaldo. He was leaning forward, his head between his hands, so lost in grief that he didn't even notice that the twins had arrived. Elizabeth slid onto a chair beside him.

"Ricky," she said softly.

Ricky looked up at her, his eyes red, his face set in pain and worry. "Liz," he said. "Thank God you've come."

Jessica sat down next to Elizabeth. "Hi, Ricky," she said very softly. "How is she?"

"I don't know," he answered, looking down at his feet again.

"What happened?" Elizabeth asked anxiously.

"She took a bottle of pills. . . . I don't know what they were," said Ricky. "I gave the doctors the bottle."

"Have they told you anything yet?"

Ricky shook his head. "I told her never mind what they'd done to her and what they were saying," Ricky cried. "But I guess it was just more than she could handle She's only a kid, you know. How much can a kid take?"

Elizabeth watched Jessica sink back in her chair, a look of panic on her face.

"I just had a terrible feeling when she was absent from school again today," Ricky continued. "I can't explain it. I felt this horrible chill go through me. I cut last period and went over to her apartment—I've visited Annie there a few times since she . . . since the tryouts. I rang the bell. I rang and rang and knocked on the door. Then I went to a pay phone and called. Why did I waste so much time?" he raged at himself.

"But you couldn't know," Elizabeth soothed, trying to calm him down.

Finally, Ricky related, he had raced back to the apartment and broken down the door. "I found her on the bathroom floor, white and clammy and not breathing. I don't know how long she'd been unconscious."

His voice cracked as he explained how he'd called for an ambulance and tried to revive Annie. "I yelled at her and shook her and prayed a lot," he said. "She mumbled something once, and that was all. Finally the paramedics got there, and we rushed right over here."

Ricky was drained by the ordeal. He sat there exhausted, yet unable to relax or let go until he knew how Annie was.

"How could they do this?" he snapped suddenly, sitting up. "What kind of stuck-up, mean kids could do this to a poor, scared girl?"

Jessica was crying now, tears running down her face.

Ricky saw her and slumped back into his chair. "Oh, no, Jess, I didn't mean it. I—you—I don't know what I'm saying!"

Jessica's sobs were audible now. She leaned her head over on Elizabeth's shoulder and wept uncontrollably.

"Stop it, Jess," Elizabeth whimpered tremulously. "You'll have me crying, too."

"I can't help it," Jessica sputtered. "*I* did this. You know I did. I'm the one who put Annie in there."

"Now, Jess, just take it easy," Elizabeth said, fighting back her own tears.

"She wanted to be a cheerleader, but oh, no! High and mighty Jessica Wakefield wouldn't let her," Jessica agonized.

Her sobs had hardly quieted when suddenly a distraught, wild-eyed Mrs. Whitman rushed into the Emergency Wing followed by her boyfriend Johnny.

"Where's my baby?" Mrs. Whitman screamed, turning wildly around toward anyone who would listen. "Where's the doctor?"

"Take it easy, Mona," said Johnny, catching up with her.

"Don't you tell me to take it easy," she yelled, pulling away from him.

A stern-faced attendant in a starched white coat walked up to Mrs. Whitman and spoke sharply to her. "Please, madam! This is a hospital."

Finding someone to direct her trouble to, Mona

Whitman grabbed the woman with both hands. "Where's my baby! What are you doing with her?"

"Who are you talking about?" the attendant asked calmly, extracting herself from the clutching hands.

"Annie Whitman!"

"Oh, yes," the attendant said. "She's in the emergency room now. They're doing all they can."

"Is she going to be all right?"

"We don't know yet, Mrs. Whitman. There's nothing to do but wait."

"Wait?" cried Mrs. Whitman. "I can't wait! Oh, my kitten! My kitten! Why did you do such a thing?"

She staggered to a chair and collapsed into it, breathing raggedly and digging into her purse. She found a pack of cigarettes and took one out with shaking fingers. Johnny lit it for her. Only then did Mrs. Whitman notice the twins and Ricky.

"Ricky," she said, jumping up and hurrying over to where he sat with Elizabeth and Jessica. Ricky, lost in worry over Annie, looked up, startled, when he heard his name. Mrs. Whitman then glanced at Jessica. "And you're a friend of Annie's, we met one night. . . ." Her sentence trailed off distractedly.

"That was me, Mrs. Whitman. Elizabeth. This is my twin sister, Jessica." Jessica lowered her head in shame, afraid to meet Annie's mother's eyes, but Mrs. Whitman had already turned back to Ricky.

"They say she tried to—they say she took . . ." Mrs. Whitman couldn't go on. Tears streamed down her face, and she put her hand to her mouth.

Ricky stood up and put a comforting hand on Mrs. Whitman's shoulder. He guided her to an empty seat next to Elizabeth and eased her into it as Johnny looked on in silence from a few feet away.

"She'll be OK." Ricky tried to sound convincing. "She's *got* to be." His words were as much for himself as for Annie's mother.

"Ricky," Mrs. Whitman said, "I'm so glad you're here."

"Ricky brought her in," Elizabeth said.

"How can I thank you, dear boy," said Mona Whitman, looking into his sorrow-filled eyes. "You've been so good to my kitten, calling her and coming to visit. You care for her, don't you?"

"Yes, ma'am," Ricky whispered.

"Can you tell me why she did this?" Mrs. Whitman shook her head vehemently. "I can't understand it."

"She did it because of the way kids treated her at school," said Ricky.

"You mean that cheerleader business?" she asked.

"Yes, mainly."

"She did mention that," Annie's mother said. "She said somebody kept her off the squad. Why would anyone do that to my kitten?"

117

Ricky looked at his feet. Elizabeth looked at Jessica, who, moving like someone who'd been drugged, wandered over to the only window in the emergency room and stared out at the hospital grounds in a daze.

It seemed like years later when a nurse walked over to them, looking frazzled and exhausted, and told them that Annie's stomach had been pumped and that she was sleeping.

"We're moving her to a room upstairs," she said.

"Is she going to be all right?" Mrs. Whitman demanded.

"We won't know that until she wakes up," the nurse replied. Then she turned away and disappeared through the heavy metal doors at the far end of the emergency room.

Mrs. Whitman and Johnny, the twins and Ricky Capaldo ended up together in the hospital cafeteria sipping coffee with little interest, waiting for news of Annie and praying fervently that she would pull through. Every conversation that had taken place earlier was repeated over and over again. The terrible question of why Annie had done it hung over them all. Jessica shrank back in the booth where they were all huddled. She couldn't look at Mrs. Whitman, or at Ricky either.

Finally they were allowed up to Annie's room. Elizabeth and Jessica trailed the others down the long, antiseptic corridors, all too clearly remembering the time Elizabeth had been rushed here after a nightmarish motorcycle accident.

118

The girls half expected to see John Edwards, the young doctor who had been assigned to Elizabeth's case. But the man who greeted them at the door to Annie's room was older, more seasoned-looking.

"I'm Dr. Hammond," he said.

"I'm her mother," said Mrs. Whitman. "How is she?"

Dr. Hammond betrayed no emotion. "I wish I could tell you everything is fine, but we just don't know yet. You can't tell me how long she was unconscious before the ambulance arrived?"

Ricky stepped forward. "I found her, Doctor. But I can't say how long she'd been out. I just don't know."

Mrs. Whitman, Johnny, and Ricky entered the room and rushed to Annie's side. Mona Whitman took hold of her daughter's limp hand. Elizabeth and Jessica moved to the foot of the bed, looking at the pale figure stretched out in front of them. She seemed lifeless, and there wasn't a trace of color in her face. Jessica felt faint. She reached for the metal guard at the end of the bed to steady herself. The twins looked on in silence for a few minutes, and then Elizabeth ushered her sister back out of the room to a waiting area halfway down the hall, where they sat quietly.

Ricky came out and paced the hallway, then went back into Annie's room. Time crawled by.

Suddenly Mrs. Whitman's cry pierced the sterile air. She darted out into the corridor. "Doctor! Nurse! Somebody! My kitten's awake!"

119

"Doctor Hammond, room four-fifteen—stat. Dr. Hammond, room four-fifteen—stat," a voice crackled over the loudspeaker. In a few minutes Dr. Hammond came striding swiftly toward Annie's room. He asked Mrs. Whitman, Johnny, and Ricky to step out for a moment.

"What did she say?" Ricky asked Mrs. Whitman as they joined Elizabeth and Jessica in the waiting area.

"She moaned and said something I couldn't understand," said Mona Whitman. She lit another cigarette and puffed nervously.

When Dr. Hammond came out of the room, his face was set in an unhappy frown. "She should be coming around much better than she is," he said worriedly.

"Is she conscious?" Mrs. Whitman asked.

"She slips in and out. Right now she isn't conscious."

"When will she be all right again?" Mrs. Whitman pressed.

"I wish I knew," he said. "When people try to take their own lives, they often don't want to be brought back. When you catch them in time, as in this case, they have another chance. But they have to want that chance, you see."

"What do you mean, Dr. Hammond?"

He seated himself on the couch in the corridor and drew the grieving woman down beside him. "Mrs. Whitman, I don't know why your daughter did this to herself, but she seems to have no will to live."

Twelve

No will to live . . . no will to live. The words echoed mercilessly in Jessica's head as she raced down the halls of the hospital. Frantically she pushed through the front door, bursting out into the night air, gasping for breath. She ran across the circular driveway at the hospital's front entrance and continued across the wide, plush lawn. She felt her throat closing up, her breath short, her blood rushing wildly.

No will, thought Jessica. *And all because of me.* Her legs shook. She ran a few more steps and then collapsed onto the soft grass, next to a little Japanese rock garden. She gulped in huge breaths of the early evening air.

I'll go away, Jessica told herself in agony. *I'll get a bus to Los Angeles, and then a plane to . . .* She buried her face in the grass, tears wetting the earth beneath her.

"Jess! Jessica!"

She heard the call faintly and looked up to

see Elizabeth coming across the lawn toward her.

"What are you doing out here?" Elizabeth said as she hurried over and wrapped her sister in her arms.

"Leave me alone."

"Are you all right?"

Jessica's response was an uncontrollable wail. Of course she wasn't all right! She would never be all right again.

Elizabeth gently rocked her twin in her arms. Jessica's sobs grew softer, punctuated by deep, long sighs. Finally she was quiet.

"Running away like that can't possibly change things or help Annie." Elizabeth's voice sounded tired. "And neither can blaming yourself. Why don't you stop?"

"I can't. It *is* my fault. Oh, Liz, I didn't know she wanted it so badly. Really I didn't! I wish I were dead!" Jessica kicked the ground, and tears fell afresh as hours of pent-up despair poured from her.

"C'mon, Jess," Elizabeth crooned, not knowing what else she could say.

"How can I be such a selfish, spoiled, impossible, vindictive—"

"Hey, hey," Elizabeth murmured. "You're talking about my favorite sister."

Jessica sat up and dabbed at her eyes with the edge of her shirt. "You heard Ricky. He's right. I *am* stuck-up and cruel. But I didn't know she wanted it so much!"

Jessica sniffled and looked pleadingly into her

122

sister's calm eyes. It was very difficult to lie to Elizabeth when she looked at her like that.

"Oh, OK, maybe I did know. Or I should have known. After all, *I* wanted it that much when I was trying out."

"You did what you thought was right," Elizabeth said.

"Yes, and put Annie where she is now!" Jessica bowed her head once more. "What am I going to do?"

"I wish I had an answer," Elizabeth said truthfully. "The doctor said she just doesn't want to live. If we only could get her interested again . . ."

Jessica suddenly jerked around and faced her sister. She stopped drying her eyes and grabbed Elizabeth by the shoulders.

"That's it!" Jessica said with determination, standing up and pulling her twin up with her. "Sure, Liz! We've got to help her!"

"That's fine, Jess, but how?"

"I'll think of something." The Jessica who could handle anything was back in form. "Come on!"

Elizabeth noted her sister's purposeful strides as she followed her back to the hospital building, through the door, and down the corridor.

"Where are we going?" Elizabeth asked, tugging at her twin's sleeve.

"I'm looking for Dr. Hammond," Jessica told the unflappable admissions nurse.

"Room one-twelve, just past the cashier's office," said the nurse.

Jessica hurried along the hall, with Elizabeth a few steps behind her. As they entered the room, Dr. Hammond was at his desk studying Annie's chart.

"Well, I thought you had gone home when Mrs. Whitman did," Dr. Hammond said gently.

Jessica sat down across from him, and Elizabeth sat beside her.

"Doctor," Jessica said, "do you think it would help to know what made Annie do this?"

"Well, it might. Do you happen to know?"

"Yes, sir," said Jessica. "*I* caused the trouble. It's all my fault."

Dr. Hammond looked doubtful. He studied Jessica's tired, tearstained face and then looked at her twin sister, also drawn and bleary-eyed. "Hmmm, is that so? And just how are you to blame, young lady?"

Jessica poured out her story in a great, cascading waterfall of self-accusation. She described herself with every vile, vicious name she could think of. By the time the unhappy story was told, Jessica Wakefield had unmasked herself as a horrific criminal, fit only to be put before a firing squad at once.

"I see," Dr. Hammond said at last. "And you believe your rejection of Annie led her to this?"

"I'm sure of it," said Jessica. "I don't know how I'll ever be able to live with myself."

Dr. Hammond pressed his hands together and stared at Jessica for a long time. "Do you really want to help Annie?" he asked at last.

"Oh, yes, if I can," said Jessica. "That's why I came to you."

"I don't know," he said slowly. "Perhaps . . . it's possible. Now, Jessica, you must tell me something. Are you willing to have Annie on the cheerleading squad? If you aren't, then please say so right now. It would be terrible to raise her hopes and then let her down again. That could be quite traumatic."

Jessica squeezed her eyelids closed, trying to hold back the tears and keep control. Elizabeth leaned over and held her hand.

"I never should have kept her off," Jessica said. "Sure, I'll make her part of the squad if that will help."

Dr. Hammond shook his head sadly. "There's no guarantee, Jessica, though it's worth a try. But I know this: Unless you mean it, Annie will get hurt all over again. You must convince her that you really want her. And you've got to be absolutely certain of it yourself."

The low murmur reached them as they were about to enter Annie's room.

". . . I know exactly how you must feel, Annie. I know what it's like to be on the outside, too," said the soft voice. "Good old Ricky Capaldo. The short, funny-looking guy. Always good for a laugh. But, Annie, it wouldn't matter what people thought if I had you. You've got to wake up. I promise, I'll never let anyone hurt you again. Annie, please. . . ."

Dr. Hammond peered around the door and cleared his throat as he and the twins stepped into the room.

Ricky glanced at them as they entered, then turned back to Annie. "Hi," he said.

"Has she stirred?" the doctor asked.

Ricky shook his head sorrowfully.

"Let me talk to her," Jessica said, crossing to the bed.

"You?" Ricky took his eyes off Annie just long enough to give Jessica a look of astonishment.

"Sure, me," Jessica replied. "It's all my fault, isn't it? I'm the one who caused this whole mess, didn't I?" She glared at Ricky and then at Dr. Hammond and Elizabeth, as though challenging any one of them to deny her overwhelming guilt. She pulled a chair up beside the bed and took Annie Whitman's pale, limp hand in hers.

"Annie," she said anxiously, "Annie, it's me—Jessica. Jessica Wakefield."

Annie didn't stir.

"Annie?" Ricky joined in. "It's Jessica! She's come to talk to you!"

Jessica turned her head away wearily. "She can't hear me," she told Dr. Hammond.

"Don't give up," he encouraged her.

Jessica turned back to the still figure on the bed. "Annie, listen, I came to see you because I've got news. Important news. You see, a huge mistake was made. When the notes were given out, things got mixed up!"

"I'm to blame for that, Annie," Ricky put in, catching on to Jessica's plan. "Don't quit on us just because a dumb, stupid manager messed up."

Elizabeth listened quietly, sensing Ricky's deep love for Annie. Up until then, no one had realized just how deeply he cared, maybe not even Ricky himself.

"You hear that?" Jessica was saying. "Ricky needs you to come back, too. But don't believe him when he says that it was his fault. It wasn't. It was the fault of somebody who was too stuck-up to see that someone can change by wanting to be better."

The voices continued as Dr. Hammond slipped out of the room to make arrangements for Ricky and the Wakefield twins to remain past the official visiting hours. Annie's last hope lay in her visitors, and the doctor knew that their presence and their words might make the difference between life and death.

Elizabeth stirred as slanting shafts of dawn fluttered across her closed eyelids. She felt a dull ache in her body and realized she was curled up in a chair in a hospital room. As she awakened, she heard a soft voice. Jessica's voice.

". . . because, you see Annie, if you don't make it, it will be my fault—and I couldn't live with that. So you've got to come back, or else it will be two of us going. Can you hear what I'm saying?"

Elizabeth slowly focused her eyes. Ricky Capaldo was leaning forward in his chair, silently watching Annie, his face close to hers. Next to him, Jessica knelt on the floor, pressed up against the bed, Annie's hand in her two, prayerful hands.

"Maybe I haven't made it clear," Jessica went on, "but we've decided to enlarge the cheerleader squad to eight. You're the eighth cheerleader, Annie, and we're all counting on you. Now, this is no fooling, Annie; it's the absolute truth!"

Elizabeth listened for more, but Jessica had fallen silent, her head slumped against the edge of the mattress. Elizabeth stood up and tiptoed over to the other side of the bed, where Jessica had kept her nightlong vigil.

"Jess?"

Jessica's head popped up, and she looked with hopeful anticipation at Annie Whitman's face.

"It's me, Jess," Elizabeth whispered, coming closer.

"Oh. I thought it was Annie," Jessica said helplessly. "It's no use, Liz. I can't bring her back. She hates the sound of my voice."

Ricky and Elizabeth watched as Jessica let Annie's hand slip away. Silent tears rolled down Jessica's cheeks. Elizabeth had never seen her twin sister so totally defeated.

Thirteen

Somewhere deep in her pool of fright and loneliness, Annie Whitman had found an anchor. Something held her, kept her from drifting beyond the horizon of infinity. Desperately she had clung to that anchor and struggled to listen to a faint voice that reached her as though through the depths of the ocean. Through the long night, Jessica's hand had kept her from slipping into the total blackness. Jessica's voice had comforted her.

Now, suddenly, the hand was gone. The voice faded. She had to look for it.

Ricky saw it first. "Jessica!" he cried.

"What?"

"Look at her hand. I think she moved!"

It moved again, ever so slightly.

"Where are you?" a faint voice pleaded. "Please . . . Jess. . . ."

Jessica felt an explosion of triumph deep inside, and a warm gush of hope came flooding back through her. Gently she took Annie's hand, and this time she felt a feeble pressure.

"She's squeezing my hand," Jessica said in wonder.

"Is it—true?" the quiet voice said haltingly.

"What, Annie?"

"Eight cheerleaders? . . ."

"Oh, yes," Jessica said. "Yes, indeed! Eight cheerleaders! Eight, including you, Annie. And we've got a practice coming up on Thursday! That's only two days from now."

Elizabeth slipped out of the room and hurried to the nurse's station.

"Could you call Dr. Hammond?" she asked excitedly. "Annie Whitman is awake!"

Elizabeth raced back to Annie's room to find the pale-faced patient sipping water through a bent straw as Ricky held the water glass for her. Jessica seemed to have shaken off her exhaustion as though by magic.

"And then there's the Pendleton game! The Pendleton Tigers always have a really terrific cheerleading squad, but we're going to leave them in the dust. You just watch!"

"You think so?" Annie replied weakly, smiling up at her squad co-captain.

"I know so," Jessica declared. "Haven't we now got two cheerleaders who can do flips? We're going to work out a whole new routine around you and Maria."

Annie glanced around at Elizabeth. Then she looked back at Jessica and Ricky.

"How long have all of you been here?" she said softly. "How long have I been here?"

"Never mind that," Ricky said. "The important thing is that you're not going to be here much longer."

Annie reached a shaky hand toward Ricky. He moved closer and took it. Annie reached her other hand to touch Jessica's. "Thank you, both of you," she said in a feeble voice. "You really saved my life."

Jessica smiled broadly. Oddly enough, despite the long, exhausting hours she had spent beside Annie's bed, she felt wonderful and invigorated.

Moments later, in walked Dr. Hammond, looking very friendly and energetic. He immediately drew the curtains back so that light flooded into the room.

"Well, well," he said, moving over to Annie's bed and taking her wrist to feel her pulse. "What's happened here?"

"Are you the doctor?" Annie asked, looking up at him.

"No, no, not at all," Dr. Hammond said. "I'm only the assistant here. These three are the doctors."

"What happened?" Annie asked.

Dr. Hammond studied her face. "You don't recall?"

"Not very much."

The doctor smiled. "Well, it will come back to you. Just remember, you have good friends who care about you."

"Don't worry," Annie said faintly. "I'll never forget that."

"How do you feel?" he asked.

"I don't know. Weak. Hungry."

"Hungry, you say? Well, then, let's get you some breakfast." Dr. Hammond was actually grinning by now.

But Annie had stopped listening to him. Instead, she was looking toward the door, blinking, trying to focus on someone who had just entered and was standing in the shadow of the doorway.

"Mom?" Annie said hesitantly.

Mrs. Whitman walked quickly to the bed and bent over to hug her daughter. "Yes, darling, it's me," she said. "Thank God you've come back to us."

Mona Whitman sat on the edge of the bed, smiling, tears of relief trickling down her cheeks.

Annie glanced toward the empty doorway. She looked back at her mother, studying her smartly tailored blue suit, the smooth hands that held her own, the beautiful face. Mother and daughter held each other's gaze for several minutes. It was almost as if they were seeing each other for the first time. Finally Annie broke the silence.

"Where's . . . you know?" she asked, looking once again toward the doorway.

"Johnny won't be around anymore, honey," said Mrs. Whitman, her eyes clear and level now as she touched her daughter's face.

"He's gone?" Annie said, her face brightening.

132

"Never mind that," Mona replied. "It's going to be you and me from now on."

"What happened, Mom?"

"Annie, you might say the roof fell in on me. When you did this—when this happened—and I didn't have any idea why! Well, that's when I realized how far we had drifted apart. I'm sorry, Annie. I hope you can forgive a selfish, blind mother."

Annie rose in her bed for the first time, sitting up to clutch her mother around the neck. She held on for dear life until she felt her mother's strong arms around her, holding her.

"Oh, Mom," cried Annie. "Mom, I love you!"

"I know, honey," Mrs. Whitman said, slowly easing her daughter back down onto the bed. "I love you, too."

"How could I have done such a thing, Mom?" said Annie suddenly.

"You wouldn't have, if I'd been there for you to talk to," Mona Whitman said.

Dr. Hammond made a move toward Annie and her visitors then, indicating it was time for Annie to rest. "I think we've had enough excitement for one morning," he said. "Our patient needs some breakfast, and then I believe she'll want to sleep."

"Please, Doctor," Annie begged, interrupting him. "Just a few moments more. Jessica . . . Ricky!"

Jessica and Ricky came over by her bed.

"Listen, I want to thank you again for pulling me through. It's coming back to me, what happened. I want you to know that I think I can make it now, without the cheerleading. Elizabeth told me not to put too much importance in it. You were right, Liz," she said. "I've got something more important now." Annie smiled, gazing at her mother.

"Oh, but we want you on the squad," Jessica insisted.

"Hey, you bet," Ricky said.

"You don't have to now," Annie said.

"Listen," Jessica said, drawing herself up. "If you're not on the squad, I'm quitting!"

"Quitting? Jessica—you? The co-captain? Oh, no, you can't do that," Annie said.

"Well, then," said Jessica. "That's that!"

"Yes, and that's all for today, too," said Dr. Hammond, shooing them all out. "You can come again this afternoon.'

" 'Bye, Liz," Annie said, " 'Bye Jess, Ricky . . . 'bye, Mom!"

Walking down the hall toward the elevator, Jessica turned to Elizabeth and said with a big smile, "Hey, you know what? I'm hungry, too! Let's stop off for brunch on the way home."

"You're on," Elizabeth said. "You earned a pancakes and eggs breakfast with all the trimmings, and I'm buying! Gee, Jess, you were wonderful!"

"Really?" said Jessica.

"Really."

"OK. You drive to the diner, and on the way you can tell me how I was! And don't leave anything out."

Elizabeth laughed. "Jessica, you are too much!"

That afternoon the twins and Ricky returned to visit their patient and found a smiling, pretty Annie sitting up and looking almost like her old self.

"Mom brought me this kimono." She giggled. "Isn't it terrific?"

"It really is," Elizabeth agreed.

"Well, since she's got that neat kimono," Ricky said, "she might not want this."

In his hands Ricky held a large cardboard box with an immense red ribbon around it.

"What is it?" Annie asked eagerly, her eyes wide.

"You probably don't even want it now," Jessica teased.

"You guys better show me what that is before I scream," Annie threatened laughingly.

Ricky put the box on the bed, and Annie's hands attacked the ribbon feverishly. Off came the ribbon, and she snatched the cover off the box.

"Ohhhhhh!"

There it was, all red and white. A Sweet Valley High cheerleader sweater.

Annie looked at it for a moment, frozen as though afraid to touch it. Then she snatched it up fiercely and clutched it to herself. She held it out at arm's length and examined it everywhere.

"Ricky, get out of the room," Annie squealed.

"What?"

"Out!" she ordered.

Out went Ricky, and the giggling girls made short work of removing Annie's kimono and getting her into her cheerleader sweater. She grabbed her hand mirror and examined herself with satisfaction.

"Can I come back in?" Ricky yelled, rushing back through the door.

"How does it look?" Annie asked proudly.

"Perfect," he said. "Just perfect!" He walked to the window, looked out for a moment, and then came back to Annie.

"OK, Whitman," Ricky barked officially. "Now, as squad manager, I'm giving you your first order. Get out of that bed and get over here to the window."

"What?" said a puzzled Annie.

"You heard me!" Ricky snapped. "Jessica, Liz . . . help her."

Mystified, Elizabeth and Jessica helped the still unsteady Annie out of her hospital bed and supported her as they moved to the window.

Ricky waved his arms above his head.

Looking out of the window, Annie saw them spread across the hospital's great front lawn in formation. Robin Wilson, Helen Bradley, Jeanie West, Maria Santelli, Cara Walker, and Sandra Bacon—the entire Sweet Valley High cheerleading squad.

At Robin's signal, they all let go with their loudest yell ever:

"Get well, Annie!"

"Oh, my goodness," Annie said. "I'm going to cry."

*　*　*

When visiting hours ended that night and Annie Whitman was well on her way to recovery, Jessica and Elizabeth hurried to the hospital parking lot and climbed into the little red Fiat.

"Come on," Jessica ordered her sister. "Let's get this heap moving! This is D-Day!"

"I know it is," Elizabeth replied. "Just don't be in too much of a hurry. We don't want Decision Day to turn into Disaster Day."

Elizabeth started the little convertible and headed out of the hospital onto Walton Boulevard, whipping around for home.

"Well?" said Jessica. "Who's going to New York, and who's going to stay here and show Suzanne Devlin around?"

"You tell me," Elizabeth said.

"I wish I knew. Let's get home so we can both find out."

Elizabeth, with uncharacteristic impatience, pushed her foot down hard on the accelerator, and the red Fiat Spider zoomed toward the Wakefields' house.

Two weeks in New York City for one twin and two weeks showing off the fabulous, glamorous Suzanne Devlin of New York, Paris, and London! Both girls were filled with anticipation as they pulled into the driveway, jumped out of the car, and raced toward the house.

Both twins get more than they bargained for in Sweet Valley High #11, TOO GOOD TO BE TRUE.

Coming Soon . . .

Watch for the
SWEET VALLEY HIGH/SOAP OPERA
CELEBRATION CONTEST

Here's your chance to win an exciting all-expense-paid trip to New York City for three.

If you're one of the lucky winners . . .*

> You will take in the fabulous sights of New York, see a Broadway show, and visit a top beauty salon for a complete makeover!

> You will spend time on the set of a major soap opera and dine with a soap star!

> You will meet the creator of Sweet Valley High, Francine Pascal, in the elegant surroundings of one of the finest restaurants New York City can offer!

Watch for complete contest details at your local bookseller starting August, 1984!

*There will be two winners—one from the United States and one from Canada. The contest will apply only to Canada, the Continental U.S., Alaska and Hawaii.